and the Great Wall of Trudd

Poog

Gax

Akiko

Mr. Beeba

Spuckler

and the Great Wall of Trudd

Written and illustrated by
MARK CRILLEY

A DELL YEARLING BOOK

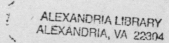

35 Years of Exceptional Reading

Dell Yearling Books
Established 1966

Published by
Dell Yearling
an imprint of
Random House Children's Books
a division of Random House, Inc.
1540 Broadway
New York, New York 10036

Visit us on the Web! www.randomhouse.com/kids

Educators and librarians, for a variety of teaching tools,
visit us at www.randomhouse.com/teachers

ISBN: 0-440-41654-X

Reprinted by arrangement with Delacorte Press

Printed in the United States of America

March 2002

10 9 8 7 6 5 4 3 2 1

OPM

For my son, Matthew

ACKNOWLEDGMENTS

First and foremost I want to express enormous gratitude to my editor at Random House Children's Books, Fiona Simpson, for simply being a joy to work with, and for the wisdom and guidance she has given me (and continues to give me) as I work on this series. Thanks as always to Robb Horan, Larry Salamone, and Joseph Michael Linsner of Sirius Entertainment, publishers of my Akiko comic books and the friendliest folks I know this side of Smoo. There are so many other thank-yous I'd like to send out, but I'll limit myself to just two more for the time being: one for my wife, Miki, and the other for my son, Matthew.

Chapter 1

The road grew narrower and narrower, with patches of incredibly tall grass creeping in from either side. The sun was right in the middle of the sky, and the air was hot and very humid. It was pretty quiet, apart from the sound of our feet on the dirt road and some weird insect noises coming from deep in the grass. I felt as if I were on a field trip or something back at the Middleton Nature Park, and I had to keep reminding myself that I was actually thousands of miles from Earth, walking along a little dirt road somewhere on the planet Smoo.

Spuckler Boach was out in front, leading the way, with his robot Gax rolling along behind him on his squeaky little wheels. Mr. Beeba and I followed, and Poog was floating in the air just above our heads.

"So tell us, Akiko," Mr. Beeba said, "what were you doing on the night Bip and Bop came to bring you here to the planet Smoo?"

"I was in my bedroom studying for a geography test," I replied, recalling all the weird stuff that had happened that night. The letter I'd received. The tapping sound on my window. The strange little spaceship floating outside, with the strange little men seated in it. It all seemed so long ago and far away. Well, it certainly *was* far away. Light-years away! But it really wasn't so long ago. Just a few days, as a matter of fact. With all the crazy stuff that had happened, though, it felt as if I'd been on the planet Smoo for *months*.

"Studying, eh?" Mr. Beeba said, sounding very pleased with me. "I had a *feeling* you were the academic sort, Akiko. Every spare moment with your nose in a book, eh? Keep it up and one day you could be an emissary of King Froptoppit, like me! You *are* planning to pursue a master's degree, I trust."

"*Master's degree?*" I repeated. "I'm only ten years old, Mr. Beeba. I'm still trying to figure out *long division*."

"You tell 'im, 'Kiko," Spuckler said enthusiastically, strutting along the road with his usual boundless energy. "You ain't no bookworm. I had ya pegged as an *adventurer* the minute I saw ya. I'll bet you were chompin' at the bit to get goin' just as soon as King Froptoppit told you about the Prince bein' kidnapped."

Ha! If Spuckler had seen how I had *really* reacted when I was asked to lead the Prince's rescue mission, he'd have had a very different first impression of me. Looking back, though, I felt glad that I'd been forced to stay on Smoo. For one thing, becoming friends with Spuckler and Mr. Beeba was fun, even if it meant spending a lot of time trying to keep them from driving each other crazy. Gax was really cool too. I mean, how many fourth-graders get to make friends with a robot? Then there was Poog. I turned and looked at him, his round purple body floating effortlessly in the air above me, his big black eyes sparkling in the midday sun. I knew that becoming friends with Poog was going to change my life forever.

"I don't know if I'd call myself an adventurer, Spuckler," I said at last. "But I've definitely had fun on this rescue mission so far. There's been some pretty scary stuff too. But plenty of fun in between."

"Now, don't rule out the idea of becoming an academic, Akiko," Mr. Beeba said, refusing to give up the idea. "Spending the day in a reference library can be every bit as adventurous as rescuing a kidnapped prince!"

Spuckler rolled his eyes and kept walking.

Chapter 2

Two or three hours had passed since we'd left the palace of Queen Pwip, and still there was no sign of the Great Wall of Trudd.

"I'd better check the map again," Mr. Beeba said, carefully unfolding the small piece of parchment Queen Pwip had given us.

"Beebs," Spuckler barked, "you've checked that thing a hunnerd times. Whatcha gonna see that ya ain't seen already?"

Mr. Beeba ignored this remark and continued studying the map, slowing his pace as he did so.

Spuckler was right. Mr. Beeba *had* already checked

the map many, many times, and he always concluded by carefully folding it back up again, clearing his throat, and making the exact same pronouncement. I wiped the sweat out of my eyes and gritted my teeth a bit as I waited for him to say it.

"Well," Mr. Beeba said after a moment, "we *seem* to be on the right road. All we can do is keep *walking*, I suppose."

"That does it!" Spuckler said, coming to a stop and spinning around to face us. "Gimme that map!"

"I will do nothing of the sort!" Mr. Beeba replied, holding the map against his chest like a child clutching a favorite rag doll.

"Give it!" Spuckler said through his teeth, bending over so that his face came down to Mr. Beeba's level. "I'm sick 'n' tired of hearin' you say the same darned thing over an' over!"

Suddenly there was a gurgly, warbly sound, and we all looked up at Poog. He was silhouetted against the pale blue sky, his big black eyes reflecting the four of us like little circular mirrors, his oval mouth chirping and whistling.

6

"Hmmm," Mr. Beeba began after a moment, scratching his head thoughtfully as he prepared to translate what Poog had just said. "Poog says you have something to tell us, Akiko."

"Me?" I asked as everyone turned to stare at me. "What? What does he want me to say?"

"He says it's time for you to tell us about the little conversation you had with Queen Pwip," Mr. Beeba explained, an expectant gleam in his eye. He looked as if he'd wanted to grill me on this subject for quite some time and had merely been waiting for Poog to give the go-ahead.

"Well, okay, sure," I said, glancing nervously at Poog. "I mean, I'd have told you all sooner, but it just didn't, um, occur to me."

Mr. Beeba and Spuckler looked at each other and smiled, clearly not believing a word I'd just said. I coughed and rubbed my forehead, trying to concentrate so I could remember everything Queen Pwip had said to me, word for word.

After a long pause, during which Mr. Beeba folded his arms and tapped his foot impatiently on the ground, I cleared my throat and began to tell them everything I could.

"First of all, she told me something about our mission to rescue Prince Froptoppit," I said, trying to recall the Seeing Room and how Queen Pwip had gazed into the strange basin of water like a fortune-teller staring into a crystal ball. "I think she could see the future of our mission."

I took a deep breath and looked out into space. Remembering all this stuff was harder than I'd thought it would be.

"Go on, girl!" Mr. Beeba said impatiently. "Don't leave us all hanging here!" I could tell he wasn't used to other people knowing more about something than he did. He was like a hungry kid waiting for me to give him a bite of my sandwich.

"Let's keep walking," I said. "It'll help me remember things better."

Poog smiled approvingly and Mr. Beeba scowled as I strode down the road, leaving them all to hurry after me. Spuckler and Gax positioned themselves on either side of me as I walked along, and Mr. Beeba scurried in front so that he could get a better look at my face, even though it meant walking backward (and occasionally stumbling in the process).

"She told me there was no need to worry," I said finally. "We'll get to Alia Rellapor's castle eventually, but it won't be easy."

"We'll *get* there," Mr. Beeba repeated, sounding like a

9

newsman taking notes for his big story, "but it won't be *easy*."

"Some fortune-teller!" Spuckler snorted. "*I* coulda told ya *that*."

"Hush, Spuckler!" Mr. Beeba snapped, clearly not wanting anything to interrupt my train of thought.

"Oh, I remember!" I said. "She warned me about a man. His name is Rock, or something like that." I knew that wasn't the exact name, but it was the best I could do at the moment.

"A man called Rock?" Mr. Beeba asked, sounding very puzzled. "A very *peculiar* name, that . . ."

"It wasn't Rock, though," I continued, walking a little faster as if to speed up my brain. "It was more like Thorp or Thork or something . . ."

There was another long pause, during which Mr. Beeba became increasingly short of breath as he struggled to move as quickly backward as I was moving forward.

"She *warned* you about this fellow, eh?" he muttered, as much to himself as to anyone else. "Oh dear. *That's* not good. That's not good at all."

"Throck!" I shouted, suddenly coming to a complete stop. "His name was Throck!"

Poog got a strange look in his eyes, a very serious look, as if the mere mention of Throck's name was troubling to him.

"Throck? You're sure?" Mr. Beeba asked anxiously, panting quite heavily now.

"Throck," Spuckler repeated. "Pretty cool name, I gotta admit."

"What else did she say about him, Akiko?" Mr. Beeba prodded. "Is he short? Tall? Stout? Svelte?" I didn't even know what the last two words meant. Fortunately I didn't really need to.

"I'm sorry, Mr. Beeba," I explained as I began to walk again, "but Queen Pwip didn't tell me what he looked like. She just told me we'd need to watch out for him."

Spuckler stepped close to my side and put his hand on my shoulder.

"Don't worry, 'Kiko," he said with a reassuring wink. "If I ever run across this Throck rascal, I'll pop him a good one right inna jaw!"

Gax clicked and whirred proudly. Even Mr. Beeba looked somewhat comforted by Spuckler's boast.

"She also said there'd be a friend," I continued, "someone who would help us out."

"A friend? Only *one*?" Mr. Beeba asked, sounding slightly disappointed. "What's his name? Or is it a she?"

"I'm pretty sure Queen Pwip said 'he,'" I said, rubbing my jaw and trying my best to remember.

"She didn't give a name, though. She just said 'a friend.'"

"Yes, well," Mr. Beeba replied, stumbling a bit over a large clump of grass, "I suppose we'll know him when we see him."

"There was one last thing," I said, glancing up at Poog as if to make sure I hadn't forgotten anything. "She said Prince Froptoppit is okay. She said he's in good health, but he's very sad and lonely. I guess he's almost given up hope of ever being rescued."

"At least we know he's all right," Mr. Beeba said, sounding very relieved.

"Well now, hang on a second," Spuckler said, wagging a finger in the air. "We don't *know* nothin'."

"*Anything*," Mr. Beeba corrected.

"Exactly," Spuckler replied, as if Mr. Beeba were simply agreeing with him. "How can we be so sure ol' Queen Pwip was tellin' the truth? What's to say her whole fortune-tellin' routine wasn't just a big hoax?"

"Spuckler!" I said disapprovingly. "Queen Pwip was so nice to us! How could you be suspicious of her?"

"I ain't bein' '*spicious* of her, 'Kiko," he protested. "I'm jus' sayin' she mighta been a big *fake*, that's all." He kicked a stone off the road with his peg leg, as if to emphasize his point.

"I'M SO SORRY TO INTERRUPT," Gax announced suddenly, "BUT IT IS MY DUTY TO ALERT ALL OF YOU TO A HUMANOID PRESENCE IN THE ROAD AHEAD."

"Humanoid presence?" Mr. Beeba repeated.

We all froze in our tracks, startled to realize that we were no longer alone.

Chapter 4

Gax continued, sounding slightly alarmed (in his own robotic way): "HE IS APPROXIMATELY SEVENTY-FIVE FEET IN ADVANCE OF OUR CURRENT POSITION. I ESTIMATE THAT WE WILL HAVE VISUAL CONFIRMATION UPON REACHING THE TOP OF THE NEXT HILL."

A shiver ran through my body and I felt the hairs stand up on the back of my neck. All at once a strange sensation came over me, a feeling that we were in very real danger. I looked at Poog. He had a terribly serious expression on his face, as if he, too, knew that something was wrong. I saw myself reflected in Poog's shiny eyes and was startled by how frightened I looked.

"You guys stay here," Spuckler said. "I'll go up and have a look."

"No, Spuckler! Don't go!" I said rather too loudly, my voice quivering.

Both Spuckler and Mr. Beeba looked at me in astonishment. I felt a bead of sweat run down my face.

"Akiko," Mr. Beeba said, putting his hand on my arm. "What's wrong? Are you all right?"

"I . . . I'm fine," I said, glancing nervously at Poog. "I just have this feeling that we shouldn't go any nearer to . . . any nearer to . . ."

"Any nearer t' *what*?" Spuckler asked, his eyebrows drawn together into a look of great concern.

"Any nearer to whatever's up there in the road ahead," I said, my voice still shaking. "It's something— or someone—dangerous."

There was a long pause as Spuckler and Mr. Beeba looked at each other, then back at me. Spuckler scratched the back of his neck.

"Look, 'Kiko," he whispered. "I ain't exactly sure what you're talkin' about, but it seems t' me that I oughta at least go up there 'n' take a *look*."

"A look," I repeated. "*Just* a look?"

"I'm just gonna take a quick peek, that's all," he said. "Then I'll come back here an' tell ya what I seen."

I looked at Poog. He still had the same serious expression on his face. He nodded very slowly.

"Okay," I said after another very long pause, glancing up the road to where it disappeared over the hill. "*But be careful.*"

Mr. Beeba, Gax, Poog, and I all watched Spuckler crawl along the edge of the road up toward the top of the hill. He crept much more carefully and quietly as he approached the point where he would be able to see the mysterious figure. My heart was pounding, and there was a part of me that just wanted to turn around and run. Instead, I bit my lip and forced myself to stand there and wait.

Spuckler stayed at the top of the hill for a minute or two, flat on his belly, before turning his head and motioning for us to join him. Mr. Beeba and I gave each other a nervous glance.

"No!" I whispered angrily. "I'm not going up there. He said he'd come back!"

"Now, Akiko," Mr. Beeba said quietly, trying to calm me down. "Spuckler is an unpredictable sort, I know, but he wouldn't encourage us to join him up there unless he thought it was perfectly safe."

I looked again at Poog but found his face oddly expressionless, as if he were leaving the matter entirely up to me.

"Okay," I said, swallowing hard. "But let's go *slowly*."

Mr. Beeba went first, Poog and I went next, and Gax followed along behind, moving as carefully as he could to muffle the squeaking noise made by his wheels. Crawling on his hands and knees, Mr. Beeba led the way to the spot where Spuckler was lying among the weeds at the side of the road. I crawled as low to the ground as I could, which unfortunately meant getting poked in the elbows over and over by all the rocks and pebbles on the road. My heart was beating even faster, and I found it very hard to breathe properly. It almost felt as if I were under water or something.

Eventually we reached Spuckler and had a clear view of the "humanoid presence" in the road. As soon as I saw him, I knew it was Throck. I felt so sure, it was as if he had the name written across his back.

Chapter 5

He was still at least sixty feet or so away, but we all got a pretty good look at him. He was six or seven feet tall, with closely cropped white hair and a large squarish head. He had his back turned toward us, so we couldn't see his face. A green camouflage uniform covered his entire body, making him look like a soldier from some alien army. The uniform had all kinds of weird tubes and bits of machinery attached to it. Every few seconds there was a loud hissing sound, as if steam needed to be regularly released from the uniform for it to function properly.

"Heavens," I heard Mr. Beeba whisper. "No *wonder* Queen Pwip warned us about this fellow."

Since Throck had his back to us, it was hard to see what he was doing. It was obvious, though, that he was *working* on something. When he was all done, he stood back and crossed his arms, as if to inspect his handiwork. There in front of him was some kind of signpost. He'd hammered it right into the middle of the road so that it would be clearly visible to anyone coming this way. Something was written on the sign in jagged little letters, but they were too small for us to read.

Suddenly Throck turned until he was almost facing us and took a few quick steps in our direction. A horrified gasp escaped from me, and it felt as if my heart was about to stop beating altogether. I watched, paralyzed, as Throck slowly looked left and right.

His face was wide and white as marble, his eyes small and pale. His mouth was concealed by a black metallic cup with several gray tubes attached to it. Each tube led to a different canister attached to his chest. He was just about the scariest-looking man I'd ever seen.

Once or twice he seemed to be looking in our direction and I was sure he'd spotted us. But then he'd continue looking left and right as if he hadn't seen us at all. He turned and looked at the sign one more time. Then he walked off the road and into the tall grasses, eventually disappearing into an area of overgrown, weedy shrubs. As he walked farther and farther away, I felt my body relax. My heartbeat slowed back down to normal speed, and it was a lot easier to breathe.

"I'll be darned," Spuckler said, raising himself to a squatting position, "if that wasn't th' feller Queen Pwip was warnin' us about."

"See?" Mr. Beeba replied. "She *was* telling the truth!"

"Well, if that was Throck," Spuckler said, jumping to his feet, "then I'm a-goin' after him!"

"No, Spuckler!" I said, grabbing hold of his arm. "Absolutely not. That man is *very* dangerous. I don't know how I know it," I added, staring Spuckler right in the face, *"but I know it."*

Spuckler looked at me with squinty eyes and a big frown. He could have kept going. It wasn't as if a little girl holding on to his arm was going to stop him. But he just stayed where he was.

"Akiko's right," Mr. Beeba said, stepping forward. "We have no quarrel with this fellow. Let him go about his business. If we're lucky, this will be the last we see of him."

I looked at Poog, hoping for some sign that this really *was* the last we'd see of Throck. Poog just stared back at me with a blank expression.

Suddenly there was a slamming noise, like a car door being shut, followed by the sound of a powerful engine firing up. The noise came from the shrubs where Throck had disappeared a moment before. The ground began to shake, and then, in the blink of an eye, a small spaceship rose out of the grasses and shot up into the sky. It moved so fast that I couldn't get a good look at it. Spuckler shielded his eyes with his hands as he watched the ship vanish into the clouds.

"That's right, Throck," Spuckler said. "Git on outta here."

After we felt reasonably sure that Throck was gone for good, we all stood up and walked down the hill to look at the sign. It read:

WARNING: THIS ROAD LEADS
TO THE REALM OF ALIA RELLAPOR.
TRESPASSERS WILL BE EXPELLED
BY ALL MEANS NECESSARY. THIS
MEANS **YOU.**

"Oh dear," Mr. Beeba mumbled, examining the dark, scraggly letters with the utmost care. "Oh dear oh dear oh dear!"

"Hey now, come *on*, people," Spuckler said in exasperation. "It's just a *sign*, for cryin' out loud. This ain't nothin' to get worked up about."

Poog's warbly gurgling voice filled the air. He continued for a second or two, then stopped abruptly. Mr. Beeba began translating almost immediately.

"Poog agrees with Spuckler," he announced, sounding as he if were surprised that anyone in his right mind would ever do such a thing. "This is indeed just a sign, and we should by no means allow ourselves to be constrained by its directives."

"Well, thank ya, Poog!" Spuckler said with a big toothy grin. "I knew the two of us'd see eye to eye on somethin' *eventually*."

Poog smiled warmly. Mr. Beeba grimaced.

chapter 6

We stepped around the sign and continued walking down the road. I felt much better, but there was still a little knot down in my stomach, a feeling that the danger wasn't completely gone. Still, it was a great relief to know that Throck had left, at least for the time being.

I tried my best to put Throck out of my mind, but it was no use. I kept wondering who he was. Was he Alia Rellapor's assistant? What was it about him that made me feel so sick and scared? And was there some sort of connection between Poog and Throck? I had a weird feeling that Poog had seen Throck before, and that he knew all kinds of stuff about him.

The road took us up and over a number of hills, and bit by bit the land began to lose a little of its wildness. The grass became shorter, and there were fewer and fewer weedy-looking shrubs. Eventually we were surrounded by beautiful rolling green hills.

"Good heavens!" I heard Mr. Beeba say. "Don't tell me that's the Great Wall of Trudd!" He was pointing beyond the hills to a thin gray line on the horizon. It was so far away that it was hard to be sure it wasn't just a long band of gray clouds in the distance.

"Wow!" I said, shading my eyes. "It looks pretty big."

"Big?" said Mr. Beeba. "It's *enormous!* It must be hundreds of miles long!" He looked as if he was making a mental calculation based on the distance and length of the hazy gray line.

"Come on, gang," Spuckler said, urging us onward. "We better pick up the pace if we're gonna get there before the sun goes down."

Spuckler was right. The wall was still many miles away, and if we walked too slowly it would be dark by the time we got there.

So we continued down the road as fast as we could, taking breaks every half hour or so. Each time we got to the top of a hill, we got a clearer view of the Great Wall of Trudd, and each time, it appeared even bigger than before. We all became so intent on moving quickly that we almost stopped talking to one another. For at least a couple of hours there was nothing but the sounds of me and Mr. Beeba panting, Gax's wheels squeaking, and Spuckler whistling some strange, almost tuneless melody. Finally, as the late-afternoon sun covered the land with a warm yellow glow, we crossed one final hill and descended a long, graceful slope that led to the base of the wall.

Chapter 7

It was huge. Huger than huge. It must have been about two hundred feet tall, maybe even taller. I have no idea how *wide* it was, since it went off in either direction as far as the eye could see, eventually disappearing over the hills into the haze. One thing's for sure: There was no way we'd be able to walk *around* the thing.

It reminded me of the Great Wall of China, except it was really different in a lot of ways. I mean, I remember seeing a picture of the Great Wall of China in my history book at Middleton Elementary, and I'd say the Great Wall of Trudd was twenty or thirty times higher. (Not that there's anything *wrong* with the Great Wall of China.

They just could have made it a lot taller, that's all.)

We all stood there in the middle of the slope, staring at the wall with our mouths open wide. It was built entirely out of roughly cut gray pieces of stone: gigantic

boulder-sized ones at the bottom and smaller, flatter ones at the top. There were towers and windows built into it, as if it was a castle and a wall at the same time. Way up at the very top there were rickety old poles with enormous weather-beaten flags waving from them. I half expected to see little soldiers up there marching back and forth, keeping watch over who knows what kind of enemy. But there was also an old, ghost-towny feeling about the place, and it was pretty obvious that no one had actually lived there for years and years.

"Look at all the windows," I said. "Do you think people used to live *inside* this thing?"

"Evidently so," Mr. Beeba replied, sounding as if he was about to come up with an elaborate theory on the subject. "Their whole society must have revolved around the maintenance of this wall."

It was pretty spooky to think of thousands of people spending their entire lives inside this wall. I couldn't help wondering what had happened to them all.

"Well, if they made windows," Spuckler said, rubbing his jaw with one hand, "they must've made *doors,* too."

"Good thinking, Spuckler," Mr. Beeba replied. "If we can find a door, maybe we can locate some sort of passageway from one side to the other."

So we walked down the hill until we got closer to the base of the wall and started looking for a door. Spuckler pressed a button on Gax's body, causing a binocular-like device to pop out from inside him with a loud squeak. Gax positioned the device in front of his eye sockets and began surveying the wall from left to right.

In the meantime Mr. Beeba paced back and forth, mumbling to himself as if he was making a series of very difficult calculations. Poog also seemed to be thinking about something, but he had a distant look in his eyes, as if he was focusing on something else, something many miles away.

"I'VE FOUND A DOOR, SIR," Gax announced after a minute or two of searching. "IT'S APPROXIMATELY 547 YARDS DUE EAST."

"Good work, Gax," Spuckler said, patting him on the helmet like a proud dog owner. "C'mon, gang. Let's go check it out!"

So we followed Gax through the overgrown grass

and piles of unused stone until we came to a large gray doorway. It was a very grand double-doored entrance, with a large, wide staircase leading up to it. But for some reason it was covered from top to bottom with large boards that had been firmly nailed into place, making it look like an old abandoned house or something.

"Bad luck," Mr. Beeba said. "We'll have to keep looking for another entrance."

"Oh no we *won't*," Spuckler declared as he ran up the steps and began tugging violently on one of the boards with both hands. "Your problem, Beeba . . . *rrrgh* . . . is ya give up on things . . . *nnngh* . . . too easily!"

KRRRAK!

Off came one of the boards, and Spuckler casually tossed it aside, nails and all.

"Um, Spuckler," I said cautiously, "do you need any help?" I wasn't so sure my little arms would make much of a difference, but I thought I should at least try.

"Naw, 'Kiko," Spuckler answered with a loud grunt. "I 'preciate . . . *arrrgh* . . . ya askin', though!"

GRRAAK! BRRROTT! KRRRUK!

One by one Spuckler tore the planks away, throwing them over his shoulder without even bothering to see where they'd land. The more wood he pulled off, the more the door seemed to be bulging outward, as if something was pressing up against it from the inside. It occurred to me that maybe these doors hadn't been boarded up to keep people from getting *in*, but rather to keep something inside from getting *out*.

"Spuckler!" Mr. Beeba called out, ducking his head to avoid a piece of wood Spuckler had just sent whizzing through the air. "Stop for a moment, will you? I think there's a very good *reason* these doors have been boarded shut!"

It was too late, though. The doors began to creak and groan, and the last few planks started to crack and pop off by themselves. Spuckler finally got an idea of what was about to happen and slowly started backing away.

"Stand back, everybody!" he shouted. By that time, though, Mr. Beeba and I had already stepped back at least twenty feet or so. Even Gax had wheeled himself away several yards, and Poog was floating a safe distance up in the air. Spuckler leaped out of the way just in time.

BRRRRRRRRUMMMMMMMMMMMMMMMMM!!!!

All at once the doors flew open and out came an avalanche of stone and sand. Mr. Beeba, Gax, and I continued backing away as wave after wave of the gravelly gray rocks poured out of the doorway, over the steps, and onto the grass. If Spuckler had waited any longer he would have been buried alive!

A minute or two later the last of the rocks came tumbling out, and all that was left was a huge

cloud of white dust hanging in the air. Only a tiny sliver of space remained between the top of the doorway and the mountain of stones that had just poured out of it.

"Well, I'll be gol-*darned!*" Spuckler exclaimed, scratching his head with one hand. "They went and filled the thing with *rocks!*"

"They did nothing of the sort, Spuckler," Mr. Beeba stated authoritatively. "This wall is simply so old it's disintegrating from within."

All at once I had an image of what it must be like inside the wall, with every ceiling and floor ready to cave in at the slightest footstep.

"Well, in that case," I said, adopting my best leader-like tone of voice, "I don't want anyone going in there. It's *way* too dangerous." There was a moment of silence as we all looked at one another, trying to think of what the next step would be.

Finally Spuckler cleared his throat and spoke.

"The way I see it, there's only one way we're gonna get past this thing," he said, shielding his eyes from the sun with one hand as he looked up at the very top of the wall, "and that's by climbin' *over* it."

Chapter 8

Spuckler took charge of the climbing plans, with Mr. Beeba as the self-appointed naysayer. I sat down and rested on the grass while the two of them bickered about how best to scale the wall. Finally they came up with a plan they could both agree on. Sort of.

"First thing we gotta do is tie ourselves together," Spuckler said, pulling a large quantity of rope from a compartment inside Gax and tying one end of it around his own waist. He then tied the middle of the rope around my waist and handed the other end to Mr. Beeba, who tied it around himself as best he could.

"This way if one of us falls, the other two can pull

'im back up," Spuckler explained in a tone of voice that was probably supposed to reassure us.

"Sounds like a recipe for *disaster*, if you ask me," Mr. Beeba moaned.

"You prefer goin' it *alone*, Beebs?" Spuckler barked, squinting angrily.

"Er . . . maybe I need to tie this knot a little bit *tighter*," Mr. Beeba whimpered, busying himself with the rope.

Meanwhile, Gax had produced three suction-cupped legs, which allowed him to scale the wall almost effortlessly. He scampered up and down the wall for practice, making a series of little popping sounds as he did.

"Wow, Gax," I said. "You're better at going up walls than any of us!"

"IT'S NOTHING SPECIAL, MA'AM," Gax replied modestly. "MOST ROBOTS OF MY GENERATION ARE CAPABLE OF WALL CLIMBING. THESE SUCTION CUPS WERE INSTALLED AT THE FACTORY, AS A MATTER OF FACT."

I tried for a moment to imagine the factory where Gax had been built. It must have been a pretty interesting place.

"Now, there's just one rule b'fore we start," Spuckler said, staring first at me, then at Mr. Beeba. "*Don't look down. It'll make ya dizzy.*"

The two of us nodded and tugged nervously at the rope, checking it once more.

Finally it was time to start climbing. Spuckler took the lead, I went next, and Mr. Beeba was underneath me at the bottom end of the rope. Gax followed Mr. Beeba, and Poog just sort of floated alongside us, two or three feet from the wall.

Before long we were almost thirty feet from the ground. Then forty. Then fifty. The stones were cut very roughly, so there were plenty of little ledges to hold on

to. At certain points it was no harder than climbing a steep flight of stairs. At other times it was a lot trickier than that. There was one spot where most of the wall was covered with a damp, greenish yellow moss, and every time I thought I had a solid footing my shoes would suddenly slide off to one side, leaving me clinging by my fingertips.

Spuckler definitely could have climbed a lot faster if he hadn't been tied to me and Mr. Beeba. As it was, he forced himself to go very slowly. He also called down little warnings to us as we went along, like "It gets a little steep up here, 'Kiko!" and "Watch out for the loose rocks over here on the right, Beebs."

The higher we went, the stronger the wind became. Every once in a while a powerful gust would whistle past and I'd find myself digging my fingernails into the wall with all my might. My skin was becoming all goose-pimply and I started to get a weird, queasy feeling in my stomach.

"Come on now," I said to myself. "You can *do* this. Don't be a baby."

Chapter 9

I tried not to look down, but I couldn't help myself. I really wanted to see how high up we were. Once I snuck a quick glance down and was amazed to see how far away the ground looked. I could see the doorway with all the rocks piled in front of it, but now it looked really tiny, like the entrance to a toy castle.

It reminded me of the time my parents took me to the top of this supertall building in Chicago where I could look out the windows and see all the tiny little people and taxicabs and stuff hundreds and hundreds of feet below me. Only now I didn't have a big, thick piece of glass to look through.

When we reached a spot seventy or eighty feet from the ground, Spuckler practically *ordered* me to stop looking down.

"I'm tellin' ya, 'Kiko: Ya gotta keep your eyes on the wall in front of ya," he said in a very stern voice. "It's the only way t' keep yourself from gettin' dizzy."

"Indeed," Mr. Beeba added, for once agreeing with Spuckler, "if you keep looking down you're going to get a nasty case of vertigo. Trust me, Akiko. I'm highly susceptible to dizzy spells myself!"

I knew they were right. I promised myself to stay focused on the climbing.

By this time we were nearly a hundred feet up in the air. Sweat was dripping down my forehead and getting in my eyes. I probably should have asked Spuckler and Mr. Beeba to stop so that I could take a rest, but I didn't want them to think I was some kind of weakling or something. So I just kept going, reaching up to one stone and then another, pulling myself up again and again until my whole body ached.

A minute or two later I accidentally cut my arm on a sharp piece of rock sticking out from the wall.

"Oww!"

It was a pretty bad cut. I stared with surprise as bright red blood began to run down my forearm.

"You okay, 'Kiko?" Spuckler asked, turning his face toward me to see what had happened. For some reason I turned my arm away so that he wouldn't be able to see the blood. I guess I just didn't want him to worry about me too much.

"Are you hurt?" Mr. Beeba asked, looking up from where he was a few feet below me.

"Don't worry, guys," I replied, trying my best to sound casual and unconcerned. "I just scraped myself a little. It's nothing." There was a weird little quiver in my voice, though, and suddenly my head felt . . . I don't know, *cloudy* or something.

I looked up and was relieved to see the top of the wall coming into view. I could even hear the flags up there, flapping like crazy in the wind.

"See, 'Kiko?" Spuckler called down to me. "Just another fifty feet to go. Sixty, tops."

"Sixty, tops . . . ," I repeated, surprised by the faraway sound of my own voice.

Now I really *was* feeling dizzy. I looked over and saw Poog at my side. He was hovering just a foot or two from my head with a very concerned look on his face. I had to blink over and over to keep him in focus.

"Akiko!" I heard Mr. Beeba say from a few feet below me. It sounded as if he were miles away. "Aaare yoooou o-kaaay?"

Suddenly everything looked very fuzzy, and I felt as if my whole body were spinning. For some reason I found myself doing the very worst possible thing I could have done at that moment. I turned my head and looked straight down.

All I could see was a big yellow blur in place of Mr. Beeba, and there, miles below him, a strangely beautiful cloud of green.

One by one I watched my fingers let go of the wall.

" 'Kiiikohhh," I heard Spuckler's voice, but it sounded as if he were calling from the top of a mountain. "Nooooooooooooo . . ."

I felt my body tumbling through space for a second or two before suddenly being yanked very roughly. Then everything went black.

Chapter 10

When I opened my eyes the world was upside down.

My face felt very warm, and my arms were dangling above my head. Or *below* my head, rather. You see, Spuckler's safety measures had succeeded: I was now hanging upside down, with my feet all tangled up in the rope. I was about ten feet below Mr. Beeba and Spuckler, who were both holding on to the wall with one hand and pulling on the rope with the other.

"C'mon, Beebs!" I heard Spuckler say. "Put some muscle into it!" Together they were drawing me back up the wall, inch by inch.

"I'm trying, trying!" Mr. Beeba replied with a grunt.

"Hold on, guys," I said feebly. "I'll try to get my legs untangled."

I wasn't feeling so dizzy anymore, but my face was burning hot with all the blood that had rushed to my head.

"Don't move, 'Kiko," Spuckler said urgently. "We'll getcher feet untangled in a second. First let's try'n getcha turned the right way around."

Spuckler was stretching his arm down to get hold of my leg, but I was still a few inches out of reach. He pulled a little harder on the rope to bring me farther up the wall.

BBRRRRRRUMMMMM!

There was a horrible crumbling sound, and all at once the section of the wall Spuckler was holding on to completely gave way. A million bits of rock and sand came pouring down, and Spuckler scrambled desperately not to fall.

But it was no use.

With one final clawing motion of his arm, Spuckler completely lost balance and fell helplessly through the air. I watched in disbelief as he rocketed down past me, the coil of rope connecting the two of us going from taut to loose in a split second. Then the rope snapped around my ankles as the full weight of Spuckler's body yanked down on it. Fortunately my blue jeans were thick enough to protect me from what would have been a *really* nasty rope burn!

Now the climbing order was completely reversed: Spuckler was on the bottom, I was in the middle, and Mr. Beeba was on top, holding on to the wall with all his might. For a terrible second or two, poor Mr. Beeba was forced to support the weight of all three of us!

chapter 11

Mr. Beeba wheezed and groaned but somehow managed to hold on.

Luckily, Spuckler got his bearings quite quickly, and in a flash he was back on the wall. Mr. Beeba exhaled loudly as he was relieved of Spuckler's weight.

"Thanks for holdin' on there, Beebs," Spuckler said with a nervous chuckle. "If you'da let go, it woulda been curtains for all of us!"

"Yes, well," Mr. Beeba said proudly while he gasped for air, "I'll let you know when I think of a good way for you to repay me!"

Spuckler helped me get right-side-up again. And not

a moment too soon: my head felt as if it were about to pop! He also found a nearby ledge where we could all lean back and rest a little. Then he called Gax, who crawled toward us on his suction-cup legs like some kind of strange robotic insect.

"YES, SIR?" Gax asked obediently.

"How much weight can you support with those li'l suction thingies of yours?"

"I'M AFRAID YOU'VE BECOME A BIT TOO HEAVY FOR ME IN RECENT YEARS, SIR," Gax replied, anticipating his master's plan.

"Okay, forget about me," Spuckler continued with a hint of irritation. "What about Beebs?"

"TO PUT IT DELICATELY, SIR," Gax answered, sounding slightly embarrassed, "WHAT HE LACKS IN HEIGHT HE MORE THAN COMPENSATES FOR IN WIDTH AND SHEER DENSITY."

"I *heard* that!" Mr. Beeba shouted indignantly.

"All right, all right," Spuckler sighed in exasperation. "What about 'Kiko?"

"OH, SHE'D BE NO PROBLEM AT ALL, SIR," Gax replied.

"*Now* we're gettin' somewhere," Spuckler said with a smile. Then he turned to me with a very serious look in his eyes.

"Okay, 'Kiko," he said, putting a hand on my shoulder, "I know ya must be pretty scared right now, an' if you don't think you can do this, just say."

I swallowed hard, nodded, and waited for him to continue.

"What I need ya to do is grab hold of Gax an' let him carry ya up to the top of the wall. I'm gonna have him check around and find the sturdiest part of the wall for climbin', so as we won't have any more nasty surprises." Spuckler paused, looking up at the flags on the top of the wall as they flapped noisily in the wind. The sky was growing purplish as the sun began to set.

"Once you're up there," he continued, "I wantcha to take all this rope and tie it to something good and strong, and then toss the other end of it down here to me an' Beebs."

"Gee, I don't know," I said, trying to imagine me and Gax continuing the climb all by ourselves.

"You can always say no, 'Kiko," Spuckler said, his expression still very serious. "I'll come up with a diff-'rent plan if needs be. I don't wantcha tryin' to do this if ya don't feel right about it."

I sat there on the ledge, looking up at the top of the wall, wondering what to do. I didn't want to keep climbing, and I didn't want to just stay there, either. What I really wanted more than anything else at that moment was to be right back at home in my bed, snuggled under the covers, waiting for Mom to bring in a little snack for me the way she always did on days when I was sick. I could almost see in my mind what the objects on the tray would look like: a little pinkish white ceramic cup filled with green tea, and a plateful of sweet cookies from our favorite Japanese grocery store, little white cookies with black sesame seeds and . . .

"'Kiko, didja hear me?" Spuckler asked, waving a hand in front of my eyes. He had a very concerned look on his face.

"Don't badger the girl, Spuckler," Mr. Beeba said. "Clearly she wants no part of this cockamamie scheme of yours, and I must say neither do I."

"Okay, okay," said Spuckler. "I'll come up with something else, just gimme a minute. . . ."

I felt something right behind my head and turned to look. It was Poog. He was staring intently at me, smiling just a little, and . . . I don't know, it was as if his eyes were *shining* on me. There wasn't any light coming out of them, but that's how it *felt*. Slowly my body began to warm up a bit, and the goose pimples on my arms disappeared. My head started to feel much clearer somehow, and the queasiness in my stomach was almost gone. Poog continued staring at me, only now he was smiling even more than before, and it looked as if he was nodding slightly, over and over.

"Wait," I heard myself saying.

Spuckler and Mr. Beeba both turned their faces toward mine.

"I'll do it." The words came out quickly and clearly.

"Ya . . . ya will?" Spuckler asked in astonishment.

"Are you *quite* sure, Akiko?" Mr. Beeba asked, examining me like a doctor looking at a patient. "You've been through an awfully traumatic episode just now, and I must say I have strong reservations about allowing you to—"

"I'm going to do this," I said with an air of finality. "I'm the one who got us into this mess. I kept looking down even when Spuckler told me not to, and now it's time for me to do whatever it takes to get us to the top of this wall." The more I talked, the more confident I felt. It's not as if I weren't scared anymore. I was. But somehow I felt as if I could *deal* with being scared, at least for the time being.

"But, Akiko—" Mr. Beeba began.

"But nothing," I said, turning my attention to the ropes around my waist. "Let's hurry up and get ourselves untied."

Chapter 12

Spuckler grinned and busily set to work undoing
all the knots. Mr. Beeba muttered a bit with a look of
confusion on his face but then silently joined us in free-
ing up the rope. Before long I was able to climb onto
Gax, balancing myself on top of his body. His legs
creaked a little under my weight, and I instinctively held
on with all my might. Soon, though, I felt confident
that Gax would have no trouble carrying me all the way
up the wall.

"Now, don't rush yourself, Gax," Spuckler said cheerfully. "Beebs and I can sit here on this ledge all day if
we have to."

"A-and, er, Akiko," Mr. Beeba stammered, sounding like a worried grandmother, "try not to, er . . . that is to say, I do hope you'll refrain from, eh . . ."

"Don't worry, Mr. Beeba," I replied. "I've learned my lesson about looking down."

Mr. Beeba smiled apologetically.

With a rhythmic popping sound, Gax's suction-cupped legs slowly but surely carried both of us up the wall. I kept my face turned up at all times, not allowing myself to look down even once. I didn't even want to risk looking *sideways*. I glanced to my left once, though, and was pleasantly surprised to find Poog there. I guess he'd decided to float up along with us, hovering just a few inches away from me. It was very comforting just knowing he was there.

Before long the top of the wall was only about forty feet away.

"All right, Gax," I said. "We're almost there."

"I'M GOING TO HAVE TO TAKE A BIT OF A DETOUR, MA'AM," Gax said with a loud squeak. "I DON'T WANT TO RISK WALKING ACROSS ANOTHER UNSTABLE SECTION OF THE WALL."

"Sounds like a good idea, Gax," I said, nodding in agreement. I had a momentary vision of the wall crumbling away beneath us and did my best to put it out of my mind.

Gax zigzagged this way and that as he tried to find the safest route, and Poog followed along at every turn. The sound of flags flapping in the wind became louder. The top of the wall was only twenty feet away. Then ten, then . . .

I threw my hands onto a large, sturdy-looking stone above my head and hoisted myself off Gax as soon as I had the chance. A warm wind blew into my face as I scampered over the edge and onto the great wide surface covering the top of the wall. I could hear a distant chirping sound like seagulls coming from the other side of the wall, and part of me wanted to crawl across and see what was over there. But I stopped myself.

That's something we should all do together, I thought.

Chapter 13

I took the rope and began looking for something I could tie it to. A pretty big stone jutted out from the top of the wall that I figured would do the trick. Taking hold of one end of the rope, I wrapped it around the stone several times and made a knot. I remembered my dad teaching me how to tie a square knot once when we were tying up Christmas packages to mail to our relatives in Japan. He told me I'd be surprised how important it could be to know how to tie at least one good knot. Boy, was he ever right about *that*!

"Let's see, now," I said to myself while Gax looked on in fascination, "was it right over left first . . . or left over right first?" I finally decided it was left over right. In the end, though, I think I kind of invented my own knot, because I kept looping the rope around and tying it over and over.

"Well, Gax, it's not very pretty," I said, yanking on the rope as hard as I could, "but I think it'll hold."

Crawling back to the edge of the wall but not daring to look over it, I tossed the remainder of the rope into the air and let it drop to where Spuckler and Mr. Beeba were waiting. Gax peeked over and kept me informed of their progress.

"SPUCKLER'S GOT HOLD OF IT," he said with an electronic beep or two. "HE'S COMING UP FIRST.

"NO, WAIT," he continued, "MR. BEEBA'S PULLING IT AWAY FROM HIM. MR. BEEBA WANTS TO GO FIRST."

There was a long pause.

"THEY'RE ARGUING," Gax explained.

I rolled my eyes.

"OKAY, HERE THEY COME!" Gax announced at last.

The rope went taut as Gax continued to describe their progress. I found myself crossing my fingers and repeatedly checking the knot to make sure it wouldn't come undone. Finally Mr. Beeba's head popped up over the edge.

"Well *done*, Akiko!" he cried as I grabbed hold of his hands and pulled him up to safety. "I don't know what we'd have done without you!"

Spuckler hoisted himself onto the top of the wall without assistance.

"Great work, 'Kiko!" he said, running over to give me a big hug. "I never doubted ya for a minute!" He caught a glimpse of my arm and the spot where I'd cut it.

"Whoa! What happened *here*?" he asked, holding my arm up to get a better look.

"Good heavens!" Mr. Beeba cried. "You've been injured!"

"It's, uh, just a scratch," I said. It stung pretty badly, though, I have to admit.

Spuckler reached into Gax's insides, dug around for a while, and pulled out a rolled-up piece of cloth and a little spray bottle. He sprayed the cut on my arm with the bottle (which made it sting even more for a minute or two) and then wrapped it up in the cloth nice and snug. Gax and Mr. Beeba watched every step of the procedure with great curiosity. Poog just floated nearby with an approving look on his face. I smiled and kept quiet, surprised to see how gentle and caring Spuckler could be when he put his mind to it.

"Ya gotta *tell* us 'bout this stuff, 'Kiko," he said, sounding just a little like a scolding parent. "Don't keep it all t' yourself like that. Ya could end up with an infection, or somethin' even worse."

"I promise next time I will," I said.

"My *word*, Spuckler," Mr. Beeba said admiringly, "I had no idea you were so adept at treating wounds."

"Yeah, well, I've had my share of scrapes in my time, Beebs," Spuckler said with a wink.

When Spuckler had finished with my arm, I thanked him and got to my feet.

"Come on, guys!" I said. "Let's go see what's on the other side of this wall!"

We all walked slowly across the top of the wall, which was thirty feet or so from one side to the other. The closer we got to the other side, the stronger the wind became. There was a saltiness in the air, and the sound of seabirds grew louder and clearer. The sun had reached the horizon, casting a reddish orange glow on all our faces as we gazed upon the scene before us.

There, on the other side of the wall, was a dazzling

view of the Moonguzzit Sea. The wall had been built parallel to the coastline, leaving just a small peninsula of land on the other side. Gazing down from where we stood, we could see miles and miles of water gently rolling in from the horizon. There was no sign of buildings or other man-made structures of any kind.

Except one.

There, at the very end of the peninsula, was a narrow stone bridge. Not just *any* bridge, though. This must have been the longest bridge ever built! It stretched out over the water, perfectly straight, for miles and miles until it disappeared into the horizon. We all just stood there for a minute or two, taking it in.

"Heavens!" Mr. Beeba said at last. "It's the Trans-Moonguzzit Bridge! I'd always thought the stories were sheer *fabrication.* . . ."

"Man oh man," Spuckler said. "Looks like we got a lot more walkin' to do."

"We'll never get down to that bridge before night-fall," I said. "We'd better spend the night up here and save the bridge for tomorrow."

"A fine suggestion," Mr. Beeba said enthusiastically,

leaning back against a large piece of stone and folding his hands behind his head. "I could probably fall asleep right *now* if I closed my eyes."

"It's starting to get cold," I said, sitting down cross-legged and rubbing my upper arms briskly with my hands. "We're gonna freeze if we try to sleep out in the open like this."

Just then Spuckler began climbing one of the enormous wooden flagpoles that had been built into the top of the wall.

"I can't believe he's got so much energy," Mr. Beeba moaned. "I couldn't even climb a flight of *stairs* right now!"

"He's not climbing that pole just for the fun of it, Mr. Beeba," I replied. "Look!"

Sure enough, Spuckler was taking one of the flags off the pole. A minute or two later he slid back down and brought the weather-beaten old flag over to me, draping it around my shoulders like a blanket.

"Thank you, Spuckler," I said with a big smile. "This is perfect!"

I don't know if Spuckler even heard me, though. He'd already run over to another flagpole and zipped up to the top of it with the speed and precision of a circus monkey. Before long he'd brought back enough flag-blankets for everyone, even Gax, who I figure didn't even really need one.

As the sun dipped behind the horizon and the stars began to fill the sky, it was wonderfully peaceful there at the top of the wall. I folded my hands behind my head, the rest of my body cozy and warm beneath the thick cloth of the flag-blanket. Mr. Beeba bid us all good night and apparently dropped off to sleep almost immediately, leaving Spuckler and me to talk quietly as the sky grew darker.

"Spuckler," I asked, gazing up at the thousands of stars twinkling above us, "are there other planets out there like Smoo?"

"Oh, sure," he replied matter-of-factly. "Most of 'em are pretty *weird*, though."

It got very quiet. I thought I could hear the sound of the sea, the waves lapping up on the shore hundreds of feet below us. It could have been just the wind, though.

"Spuckler," I asked, "are you scared of that guy Throck?"

There was a very long pause.

"Maybe a little," he said finally. "But I won't let him scare me out of rescuin' the Prince, that's for sure."

There was another pause. I heard a flag flapping in the wind somewhere far away.

"Neither will I," I said before closing my eyes and drifting off to sleep.

Chapter 15

When I woke up it was cold and the sky was gray-ish pink. I pulled my flag-blanket around my body as tightly as I could and tried to go back to sleep. I couldn't, though. I suddenly realized how hungry I was. After all, it had been almost a whole day since we'd had anything to eat.

I rolled over and found that Spuckler and Mr. Beeba were already awake. They were sitting near the edge of the wall, having a heated debate. They were *whispering*, but it was still a debate.

"Hey, guys," I said. "What's going on?"

"Mornin', sleepyhead!" Spuckler said with a smile. "Hope we didn't wake ya."

"No, Spuckler, you didn't," I said, sitting up straight and stretching my arms out as far as they would go. "It's time for me to get up anyway."

"GOOD MORNING, MA'AM," I heard Gax say with a cheerful squeak.

I turned to find Gax and Poog just a few feet behind me.

"Good morning, Gax. Good morning, Poog," I said, rubbing my eyes. "Boy, I sure am hungry."

"You ain't the only one," Spuckler said, rubbing his belly vigorously. "I reckon I could eat a whole *stack* of Bropka steaks right now if I had the chance."

"Yes, well, we're all quite famished, to be sure," said Mr. Beeba, "but sadly, there's not a scrap of food among us, so we'd best not dwell on the matter.

"We were discussing," Mr. Beeba continued, "the manner in which we are to descend to the bottom of the wall."

"What's to discuss?" I asked. "We'll just have to tie ourselves together and climb down the same way we came up."

"My thoughts precisely," Mr. Beeba said, apparently very relieved to find me on his side of the argument. "Spuckler, however, has this outlandish notion that—"

"I think we oughta *parachute* down," Spuckler interrupted, hurrying over to me, full of enthusiasm. "I figure one of these here flags is just about big enough for the job. Why, if it works we'll be able to drop down there as gentle as a feather on a breeze."

"*See?*" Mr. Beeba said to me, as if Spuckler had just offered proof of his own insanity.

"A parachute?" I asked, trying to stay open-minded.

"Here," Spuckler explained, picking up one of the smaller flags he'd taken down from a pole the night before.

"Oh, goody," Mr. Beeba said sarcastically. "A demonstration."

"These here pieces of junk will represent you 'n' me 'n' Beebs 'n' Gax," Spuckler continued, removing four small pieces of metal from inside Gax.

"SPARE PARTS, SIR," Gax said.

"Huh?" Spuckler asked.

"I PREFER THE TERM 'SPARE PARTS' TO THE TERM

'PIECES OF JUNK,'" Gax explained, sounding slightly offended.

"Oh. Right," Spuckler said. "Spare parts. Sorry about that, ol' buddy."

Gax clicked and buzzed his approval.

"Just you watch," Spuckler said excitedly, tying the four pieces of metal to the four corners of the flag. "This is one of my best ideas yet."

A moment later he was done.

"Course, this is just a model," Spuckler continued, carrying his creation to the edge of the wall. "The real thing'll be even *cooler*."

Raising a finger in the air to see which direction the wind was coming from, Spuckler twisted his body back and hurled the flag up into the air. The wind rushed underneath it and raised it up at the center, while the four metal weights pulled it down at each corner. Slowly and gracefully, Spuckler's little handmade parachute floated over the edge of the wall and down toward the coast. Mr. Beeba and I watched in amazement while Gax popped and sputtered with pride. Poog smiled and said something in his gurgly language.

"Poog says"—Mr. Beeba translated with some hesitation—"Poog says it's a splendid idea."

"Well, hot *dang*," Spuckler laughed. "Me 'n' Poog seem to be agreein' on most everything these days."

"Hmpf!" Mr. Beeba groaned. "Well, I suppose the idea *does* have its merits."

Chapter 16

Spuckler ran off in search of the largest flag he could find. Eventually he came back with one that looked as if it would be just perfect. It was about twenty feet square and had just a few small holes around the edges. Spuckler tied one corner of it to Gax, grabbed hold of another corner himself, and instructed me and Mr. Beeba to take the other two corners. Poog observed the whole process with a look of curiosity and amusement.

We then walked carefully over to the edge of the wall and agreed that we would jump on the count of three. The only problem was we couldn't decide what jumping on the count of three actually meant.

"Look, it's easy," Spuckler said with an air of exasperation. "I'll say 'one,' then 'two,' and then when I say 'three,' we all jump."

"Yes," Mr. Beeba said, adjusting his spectacles, "but do you mean that we should jump *as you are saying* the word 'three,' or just *after* you say the word 'three'?"

"I think he means *as he is saying* the word 'three,'" I said. "Right, Spuckler?"

"I don't even know what neither of you two are *talkin'* about!" Spuckler cried.

"It's a perfectly clear distinction——" Mr. Beeba began.

Suddenly a strong gust of wind swept under the flag and began carrying us up into the air. Mr. Beeba and I struggled to stay in place.

"The wind is too strong, Spuckler!" I shouted as the flag lifted my feet off the surface of the wall. "It's going to knock us over the edge!"

"That's the whole point, 'Kiko!" Spuckler called back to me as he allowed himself to be swept away. "Go with the flow!"

Within seconds all four of us were carried up into the sky, with Poog floating along behind. The flag bil-

lowed up like an enormous mushroom, then gradually began to descend toward the sea below us. I stared in amazement at the entire length of the Great Wall of Trudd as the four of us dropped bit by bit, slowly circling around and around like a spinning umbrella.

"We're . . ." Mr. Beeba gasped, his face overcome with an astonished smile. "We're *flying!*"

"Admit it, Beebs," Spuckler called across to him, "you're havin' *fun,* aren't ya?"

The entire descent took about a minute and a half. Finally we dropped right down into the waters of the

Moonguzzit Sea, the flag settling into the waves like an enormous deflating beach ball. We all got soaking wet (well, all of us except *Poog*, that is), but fortunately no one got hurt. We made our way back to the shore, pulling the flag along with us.

"I say, Spuckler," Mr. Beeba said with a great big smile, "that was very clever of you, considering you've never studied the laws of aerodynamics."

"I make it a rule never to learn about stuff that's hard to pronounce," Spuckler replied. "Makes my head hurt."

We all agreed to rest up a little before beginning our trek across the bridge. Spuckler sat down and gave Gax a little tune-up. Mr. Beeba and Poog took a quiet stroll along the coast. Me, I just collapsed happily on the beach, closed my eyes, and waited for my blue jeans to dry in the morning sun.

Ten or fifteen minutes later, when Poog and Mr. Beeba came back from their walk, we took our first steps onto the long stone bridge.

Chapter 17

The design of the bridge was quite simple. It was about twenty feet wide, with four-foot walls on either side that served as guardrails. It appeared to be built out of the same stone that had been used to build the Great Wall of Trudd, except it looked even older and more weather-beaten.

There was enough space for all of us to walk side by side, though Spuckler tended to be out in front just because he walked so much faster than the rest of us. I kept looking off into the distance, at the spot where the bridge disappeared into the horizon like railroad tracks. I was checking to see if we would come across another one of Throck's signs, or even Throck himself. Fortunately, there was nothing to see but miles and miles of bridge.

"You know, Akiko," Mr. Beeba said as we walked along, "you've never told us much of anything about your home planet, Orth."

"Earth," I quietly corrected, trying not to embarrass him.

"Yes, of course," he said with a cough. "So what's it like on, um, Errrth?" The way he said it made it sound like a whole different planet somehow.

"Oh, it's pretty cool, Mr. Beeba," I said. "You all ought to come and visit me someday."

"We'd be delighted to," Mr. Beeba replied eagerly.

"Are there all kinds of weird *monsters* and stuff?" Spuckler asked, sounding like a schoolboy with an over-active imagination.

"No, Spuckler," I answered. "Well, at least none that *I* know of."

"Hmm," Spuckler replied with a yawn. "Sounds kind of boring."

"ARE THERE ROBOTS, MA'AM?" Gax asked. "LIKE ME?"

"Oh yeah, we've got *loads* of robots on Earth," I told him. "But not like *you*, Gax. Why, I'll bet there's no other robot like you in the entire universe!"

"Got *that* right," Spuckler said, his face glowing with pride.

Gax buzzed and squeaked happily.

Poog made a short gurgly sound, which Mr. Beeba translated as "Do you miss your parents?"

What a question!

I remembered the time my parents had to go to some sort of conference or something in Michigan. It was a school night, so there was no question of my going with them. They ended up having me stay the night at the home of one of my mom's friends, Mrs. Powell. At first I thought it was pretty cool, but then for some rea-son all the little stuff started to bother me, like the greasy chicken Mrs. Powell cooked for dinner and the weird collection of ceramic frogs she kept in her bath-room. I think I even cried a little before I went to sleep. All I wanted was to be back home with my parents.

Things were different now, though. For one thing, I was two or three years older. And sure, I still missed my parents a lot, but I also felt very *important* here on Smoo. I knew that Spuckler, Mr. Beeba, Gax, and even Poog . . . I knew they all *needed* me for some reason. It was a slightly uncomfortable feeling sometimes, as if I was having to be a whole lot more responsible than I really wanted to be. But it was also a good feeling, as if I was getting the chance to become a slightly different kind of kid.

"Yeah, Poog," I finally answered. "I miss them. I miss them a lot."

Spuckler and Mr. Beeba turned to me with concerned looks on their faces.

"I know I'm going to get to see them again, though," I continued, "just as soon as we've rescued Prince Froptoppit."

"You betcher boots ya will," Spuckler said with a smile. "I'll take ya right back home *myself* if I have to!"

"Good heavens!" Mr. Beeba interrupted with an expression of great surprise. "There's a *building* up there!"

He was right. It was still just a tiny speck in the distance, but it was clearly visible. A building. Right in the middle of the bridge!

Chapter 18

As we got closer the details of the little building became easier to see. There was a big rotating sign on top, just like you'd see at a gas station, with a strange symbol on it that looked like a word in Arabic or something. The building itself was no more than thirty or forty feet square, with a perfectly flat roof and dark-tinted rectangular windows, some of which were cracked and partially boarded up. The bridge had been specially widened to make space for the structure, and a dozen or so raggedy little flags fluttered from poles that circled the building. There were even a couple of little garbage cans, cylindrical ones with beat-up silvery covers that squeaked

noisily in the wind. All in all, I'd say it looked pretty much like a roadside diner you might find somewhere outside of Middleton, an old place that had seen better days. *Much* better days.

"Smudko's!" Spuckler said, sounding as if he'd died and gone to heaven. "Well, I'll be dad-*gummed!*"

"Here?" Mr. Beeba asked, his eyes open wide in disbelief. "Impossible! They never requested a building permit!"

I didn't have the slightest idea what they were talking about.

"Um . . . what's Smudko's?"

"It's an intergalactic chain of restaurants, Akiko," Mr. Beeba explained as we continued walking toward the building and its lazily rotating sign. "Atrocious food. Strictly a dining alternative of last resort."

"Don't listen to him, 'Kiko," Spuckler said, licking his lips in anticipation. "There ain't nothin' like a Smud Burger. Heck, two or three of 'em would go down pretty *good* right about now!"

"Don't get your hopes up, Spuckler," Mr. Beeba said, walking up to one of the windows and wiping away the soot to look inside. "Clearly this place was abandoned *years* ago for want of patrons."

"Why would they build a restaurant out in the middle of this bridge?" I asked. "There aren't any customers around for miles. I mean, come on. What did they *expect*?"

"Your guess is as good as mine, Akiko," Mr. Beeba replied, wiping an even larger section of the window clean with his gloves. "I suspect it was some sort of bureaucratic error. The Smudko's Corporation got so big that at one time they were opening restaurants at the rate of one thousand a day. Mistakes were bound to happen."

Gax wheeled himself over and joined Mr. Beeba in checking the place out. Spuckler seemed more interested in locating the front door, which he did in a matter of seconds.

"Whatchew guys *waitin'* for?" he called to the rest of us, pulling the door open with a prolonged rattling squeak. "C'mon, let's go *inside* already!"

Chapter 19

One by one we entered the old restaurant, stepping cautiously across the floor while our eyes adjusted to the darkness. The first thing I noticed was how clean the place was. I mean, it was really old and almost falling apart in certain spots, but there was hardly any dust anywhere. There were about a dozen circular tables, each with six chairs arranged neatly around it and little metallic napkin dispensers set carefully in the center. There was a kind of bar at the back with round padded stools lined up in front of it and a long shiny footrest underneath. The air smelled nice and clean, with just a hint of cooking oil or something like that.

"Well," Mr. Beeba muttered to himself, "they certainly *left* the place in good condition. I'm rather surprised that they forgot to lock the door, though."

"I'm not so sure this place is really *abandoned*, Mr. Beeba," I said, pointing at the smooth, shiny tabletops. "Somebody's been in here tidying this place up."

"Let's hope it's someone who knows where the *food* is," Spuckler said, still licking his lips hungrily.

"MY ACOUSTIC SENSORS ARE DETECTING SOME SORT OF AUDITORY DISTURBANCE," Gax reported, turning his head from left to right like a satellite dish.

"I don't hear anything," I said.

"Hush, Akiko," Mr. Beeba whispered, raising a cautious finger in the air. "We need to be absolutely silent in order to catch it."

A minute or two went by as we all stood there, trying our best to hear what Gax had picked up. Only Poog continued moving, floating noiselessly through the air as he inspected the strangely well-kept room.

Then I heard it. Coming from back behind the bar was a . . . *breathing* sound. It was low and husky and very, very slow.

Spuckler signaled to us that he would go check it out by himself. Mr. Beeba and I nodded vigorously and stayed right where we were. I tried to imagine what would make such a sound and couldn't decide if it was a human or an animal or something else altogether.

Spuckler stepped as quietly as possible over to the bar and took a peek behind it.

"Hmpf!" he snorted, sounding as if he was more amused than frightened by what he saw. He grinned and motioned for us to come over and join him.

Mr. Beeba, Gax, and I went across to the bar and, looking behind it, saw a middle-aged man with a bushy black mustache and a big potbelly, sound asleep in a comfy armchair. He had his arms draped across his chest with his fingers neatly laced together and his legs propped up on a big tin can placed carefully in front of him. That breathing sound we'd heard was now clearly a quiet, steady snore, and I had to cover my mouth to stop from giggling. He looked like a cross between Santa Claus and a hot dog salesman in a baseball stadium.

"Who is he?" I whispered to Mr. Beeba, still trying hard not to laugh.

"I don't know," Mr. Beeba whispered back. "He must be an employee of the Smudko's Corporation."

Sure enough, he was wearing a T-shirt and a little paper cap, both of which bore the same curious symbol that I'd seen on the restaurant's sign outside. His face looked so peaceful, I wondered if we shouldn't just turn around and tiptoe back outside.

Spuckler would have none of *that*, however.

"*Hey, pal!*" he shouted at the top of his lungs, his voice bouncing off the walls and filling the entire room. "*You're sleepin' on th' job!*"

Gax gave a little squeak of surprise, and even Poog whirled around to see the man's reaction. Mr. Beeba glared at Spuckler in irritation.

"You *idiot!*" he said through his teeth.

The restaurant man's face twitched and his whole body shook from side to side. Slowly his eyes fluttered open and his jaw dropped slightly. As his eyes began to focus on us, his face quickly took on an expression of great surprise. For a second or two I was afraid he'd be angry, but then a gentle gleam appeared in his eyes and he smiled from one ear to the other.

"*Customers!*" he said happily.

Chapter 20

His voice was high-pitched and squeaky, not exactly the sort of thing you'd expect to hear coming from a man his size. He thumped his feet down on the floor and stood up as fast as his body would allow him.

"You," he continued, suddenly sounding a bit more cautious, "you *are* customers, aren't you?"

"Actually—" Mr. Beeba began, clearing his throat in preparation for a lengthy explanation.

"Darn *right* we're customers!" Spuckler interrupted. "And we're *real* hungry, too!"

Spuckler was right: We *were* hungry. Well, *I* was, anyway.

The restaurant man clapped his big hands together and rubbed them gleefully.

"Oh, this is marvelous!" he said, doing a little jig. "Customers!"

I wondered how long it had been since he'd *had* customers. Months? Years? In any case, he seemed determined to make the most of the occasion.

"Please, take off your coats and sit down," he said, apparently not noticing that we weren't wearing any coats. "I'm going to fix up a feast the likes of which you've never seen!

"Sit! Sit!" he repeated as he hustled through a pair of swinging doors into what appeared to be a tidy little kitchen. The doors creaked back and forth just once before he burst back through with an apologetic smile.

"The lights!" he announced by way of explanation. "How could I forget the lights?"

He flicked a switch on the wall, quickly barged back through the doors, and vanished from sight. With a bit of flickering and buzzing, the lights on the ceiling burned bright white, making the whole room seem even shinier and cleaner than it had before. Then, after a second or two of silence, a wonderful clattering noise came forth from the kitchen, sounding more like a dozen cooks at work than just one.

Spuckler lifted Gax onto one of the stools while Mr. Beeba and I sat down next to each other. Poog just hovered near my shoulder with a contented look on his face. No one was in a better mood than Spuckler, though. He licked and smacked his lips loudly, causing Mr. Beeba to shudder with an exaggerated expression of embarrassment.

Before long we heard something sizzling and popping on a grill, and a greasy but pleasant aroma floated out from the kitchen.

"Smell that, 'Kiko?" Spuckler asked, greedily inhaling as much of it as he could. "That's what made this place famous: Smud Burgers!"

Mr. Beeba grimaced as if he'd have much preferred something along the lines of filet mignon.

I don't know why, but while I was sitting there I started thinking about the cafeteria at Middleton Elementary. The food there was generally pretty decent. Well, everything except the squishy little burritos wrapped in plastic that they served on Wednesdays. Yuck! I always tried to give mine to someone else, and if I couldn't manage that I'd just toss the whole thing right into the nearest garbage can.

Suddenly I had this ridiculous vision of the Smudko's restaurant guy coming back with a whole plateful of those very same Middleton Elementary burritos. I was so hungry, I'd have gladly eaten five or six of them! I'm not kidding, either.

Chapter 21

Soon the kitchen doors began flying open and shut as the restaurant man bustled in and out, bringing food to us by the trayful. There was a wide, round plate with big flat burgers stacked up into a miniature pyramid. A big bowl was piled high with shiny green meatballs, rubbery things that looked as if they might bounce if you dropped them on the floor. There were several little plates of fried wormy-looking stuff that may or may not have been some kind of vegetable. Next to that was an enormous football-shaped thing that looked a lot like a baked potato, but when Spuckler cut it open it was all purple and slimy on the inside. And there were

big paper cups for all of us (even Poog!) filled with a black liquid that looked a lot like something I once saw my dad pour into the engine of our car. I'll be honest: It all looked extremely unappetizing.

But the smell! It smelled *fantastic*. At least ten times as good as most of the fast-food places back in Middleton, and maybe even better than my mom's cooking.

"Eat up, folks!" the restaurant man said proudly, as if he couldn't wait to see what we thought of it. "And keep your money in your pockets," he added. "It's all on the house!"

Thank goodness. I didn't even *have* any money in my pockets.

Spuckler didn't need to be told twice. He picked up two Smud Burgers, one in each hand, and stuffed both into his mouth at once. It was a pretty impressive sight, and it made me curious to try one myself.

I'll never forget my first bite of Smud Burger. The bun was quite soft and spongy, but the meat was, well, *crunchy*! It was sort of like eating a mouthful of peanuts, except it was also very juicy, like a big, ripe tomato. There were all kinds of flavors in it, from sour and salty

to sweet and spicy. I finished the whole thing in under a minute, then started on another.

Mr. Beeba seemed more impressed with a doughnut-shaped food that was as soft and light as cotton candy but tasted a little like some sort of baked fish.

"Heavens, my good man," Mr. Beeba said, his mouth still full of food, "these are some of the finest Moolo Rings I've ever had."

"Please," the restaurant man replied with a great big smile on his face, "call me Yabby."

"Yabby," Spuckler declared, half rising to his feet, "I reckon you're the best cook in the galaxy, and I ain't jus' sayin' that, neither!"

Yabby beamed and blushed both at once. You could tell he was *very* proud of his cooking.

"So where are you folks headed?" he asked us.

"Just to the end of the bridge," I said, glancing at Mr. Beeba to make sure it was okay to talk about our mission. He nodded and waved a reassuring hand, his mouth stuffed full of Moolo Rings.

"You can tell him more if you like, Akiko," he said, swallowing loudly. "I'm sure we can trust Mr. Yabby not to tell anyone what we're up to."

"That's for sure," Yabby chuckled. "I get *very* few customers, as you've probably guessed."

"We're on a mission to rescue Prince Froptoppit," I explained. "He's been kidnapped by Alia Rellapor."

"Oh dear," Yabby said, a worried expression coming over his face. "I hope you have warm clothes."

There was an awkward pause as I tried to figure out

what he meant by this. I glanced at Mr. Beeba and Spuckler, who both gave me an *I don't know either* look in return.

"And, uh, what if we don't?" I asked Yabby.

"Well, Alia Rellapor's castle is surrounded by miles of snow and ice," Yabby explained. "Without proper clothing you'll all freeze to death before you get anywhere near it."

Spuckler turned to Mr. Beeba, pointing an accusing finger at his face.

"You never said nothin' 'bout no snow and ice!"

"Yes, well, the books *I* read on the subject were, um, more concerned with the *topography* than the climate, you see. . . ."

"Well, of all th' . . . ," Spuckler fumed. "What're we gonna do *now*?"

"Relax, my friends," Yabby said. "I'll have a look around back. Maybe I can find some coats for you."

chapter 22

Yabby went back into the kitchen and reemerged a minute or two later with his arms full of coats, blankets, and other pieces of cloth. He also produced a needle and thread and a measuring tape and began taking my measurements.

"I haven't got anything in your size, little girl," he said to me, "but I think we can work something out."

We spent the next several hours chatting about this and that as Yabby made a coat for me. Spuckler told a bunch of exciting stories about things he'd done when he was younger: rocket races he'd won, monsters he'd fought. Some of it sounded as if he was just making it all up, but it was very entertaining anyway.

Mr. Beeba went back into the kitchen and made some tea for us. It was kind of orange and extremely sweet. I didn't really like it, but I tried to drink it all anyway so he wouldn't feel bad. Unfortunately, Mr. Beeba thought this meant I really liked it, so he refilled my cup! From then on I just took tiny little sips.

I asked Yabby if he'd ever seen Alia Rellapor or the man called Throck.

"No, no, I never have," Yabby replied. "I saw a dark little spaceship fly overhead the other day. I wonder if *that* might have been this Throck fellow you're talking about.

"But no, I've never seen either of them," he added with a wink, "and I hope I never do!"

Yabby was very nearly done with my coat. He even managed to take some leftover scraps and make coats for Poog and Gax. We all complimented him on his craftsmanship as we tried our new clothes on.

"You are a man of many talents, Mr. Yabby," Mr.

Beeba said respectfully, refilling Yabby's cup with tea. "It's a shame you can't join us on our mission. We could use a man of your resourcefulness!"

"Yeah, Yabby," Spuckler agreed. "We'd love to have ya along. Ya gotta admit it'd be a whole lot more fun than hangin' around this borin' old restaurant."

"I wish I could," Yabby replied, blushing at the praise. "I'm a cook, though. Not an adventurer."

Spuckler and Mr. Beeba tried pretty hard to convince him, but it was clear he was determined to stay. So we all stood up and prepared to say goodbye.

Carrying our coats folded under our arms, we all went outside and stood in front of the restaurant for a few minutes. A cool wind swept across the bridge, making the little flags surrounding the building flutter wildly.

"Do take care of yourselves, now," Yabby said with a slightly worried look on his face. "The realm of Alia Rellapor is very inhospitable. You shouldn't stay there any longer than you have to."

"Believe me, Mr. Yabby," Mr. Beeba said, looking only slightly less worried himself, "we're hoping to spend as little time there as we can!"

"Oh dear, I almost forgot!" Yabby said, hurrying back into his restaurant. "Wait right here!"

A moment later he came back holding a large brown paper bag with the Smudko's logo on it.

"I've packed a few sandwiches for you," he explained, handing the bag to Spuckler, "for the road."

"Why, thank ya, Yabby!" said Spuckler. "I was sort of *hopin'* we might be able to get a little carryout. . . ."

I gave Yabby a big hug and thanked him for the coat, the food, and everything else he'd done for us. Spuckler and Mr. Beeba each shook Yabby's hand, and Gax said goodbye with a little nod of his helmet. Poog also thanked Yabby, which Mr. Beeba said was a pretty big deal since Poog usually remained silent in this kind of situation.

Finally we all waved goodbye and continued along the bridge, turning back every so often to wave at Yabby one more time. A half hour or so later, Yabby and the restaurant were nothing more than little dots in the distance.

Chapter 23

With our bellies full of Smud Burgers, we were all in a very good mood as we walked along the seemingly endless bridge. From the look of the sun in the sky, I figured it was early afternoon. Our goal was to make it to the end of the bridge by nightfall, but since we had no idea how long the bridge actually was, it was hard to tell how long it would take. We walked as fast as we could, though, just in case.

The longer we walked, the cooler the wind seemed to get. After an hour or two it definitely started to get colder. The sky began to cloud over, and the wind had a damp, chilly sting to it that hadn't been there before. Mr. Beeba and I put our coats on first, followed by Gax and Poog (actually, I had to help Poog put his coat on, since he couldn't do it by himself). Spuckler kept insisting that it wasn't that cold, but finally even *he* gave in and put his coat on.

The sky got grayer and grayer, making it difficult to tell how late it was. Every once in a while the sun would break through the clouds, lighting up portions of the bridge and the water in dramatic bursts of white light. The surface of the Moonguzzit Sea became dark and very rough, with choppy little waves rippling under the bridge from one side to the other. I pulled the collar of my coat up against my cheeks and blew on my hands to keep them warm.

"Mr. Yabby was right," Mr. Beeba said, half burying

his head in his coat. "We are most *definitely* heading into a cooler climate."

"Cold is good, Beebs," Spuckler said optimistically. "Gets the blood churnin'."

"THE TEMPERATURE IS FAST APPROACHING THE POINT OF FREEZING, SIR," Gax announced with a jittery clicking noise. I wondered if the lower temperatures would be hard on Gax. I remembered this big ice storm we had in Middleton one time, and how hard it was for my dad to get our car started. Gax seemed to be doing pretty well, though, and I should probably have been more worried about myself. After all, I didn't have any gloves or even a hat.

"Uh-oh," Spuckler said, pointing a finger down the length of the bridge. "Looks like old Throck's got another message for us."

"Another message?" I asked.

"I think I see another of his li'l signposts down there in the middle of the bridge."

Sure enough, there in the distance was a small wooden sign with the same scratchy writing on it, creaking back and forth in the icy wind. We all quickened our pace until we were close enough to read it. There was a part of me that really didn't *want* to read it, to tell the truth.

It said:

STOP! TURN AROUND! GO BACK!
RETURN TO WHERE YOU CAME FROM!
IT WILL SOON BE TOO LATE TO RECONSIDER.
THIS IS YOUR FINAL WARNING.

"F-final warning?" Mr. Beeba sputtered. "I don't like the sound of *that*."

"We must be getting closer to Alia's castle," Spuckler said, his breath making little white clouds in the air. "I wish old Throck would just come out and face us, 'stead of puttin' up these corny signs."

"I don't *want* to face him," I said, my voice trembling a little. "I don't ever want to see him again!"

"Don't you worry, 'Kiko," Spuckler said, placing a reassuring hand on my shoulder. "I'll protect ya. I won't let Throck touch a hair on your head."

"Yes, Akiko," Mr. Beeba joined in. "Spuckler will

protect all of us, you can be sure of that."

"Hey, I didn't say nothin' about protectin' *you*, Beebs," Spuckler said with a wink.

"Hmpf!" Mr. Beeba snorted. "Come on, let's keep moving. It's the only way to stay warm."

So we stepped around the sign and left Throck's "final warning" behind us. A few minutes later it started to snow.

Soon the entire surface of the bridge was covered with a fine dusting of white. It seemed to grow thicker by the minute, and before long there was a good inch or so of the stuff. With some amusement I glanced back at the various tracks we were making: my own waffle-textured sneaker prints; Spuckler's single footprint alternating with the little dash made by his peg leg; Mr. Beeba's enormous round footprints;

Gax's narrow, wobbly tire tracks. If someone was following us, they'd be scratching their heads trying to figure out what sort of creatures we all were!

Every once in a while the wind would suddenly die down for a minute or two. Then we would find ourselves strolling through an oddly peaceful scene, surrounded by big white snowflakes against a charcoal-gray sky. It was almost totally silent, apart from the muffled crunch of our footsteps and the soft patter of the waves lapping up against the bridge. I could almost believe that there was nothing at all to be afraid of.

"Are my eyes playing tricks on me," said Mr. Beeba as he peered through the drifting snowflakes, "or is that the end of the bridge up there?"

It was so dark that I couldn't see much of *anything*. But as we continued walking, the outline of a faraway shore gradually became visible, with the dark outline of a mountainous horizon beyond it. We walked even faster, and before long the end of the bridge was plain for all of us to see.

We'd done it. We'd made it to the realm of Alia Rellapor.

Chapter 24

"**Hot diggity dog!**" Spuckler cried, obviously very pleased with our progress. "Get ready, Alia!" he added at the top of his lungs, cupping his hands around his mouth and sending his voice echoing over the hills. "We're on our way!"

Gax buzzed and squeaked cheerfully. Even Poog had a big smile on his face.

I wasn't happy *at all*, though. I know it doesn't make much sense, but even though we'd spent days and days doing everything we could just to get here, now that we'd arrived I wanted nothing more than to turn around and go back.

"Don't worry, Akiko," Mr. Beeba whispered, almost as if he were reading my thoughts. "I'm just as frightened as you are. I've had moments when I secretly hoped we'd never even *make* it this far. But I'm sure that in the end everything will be okay."

"Really?" I asked. "You promise?"

"Well, er," he replied, gesturing nervously with his hands, "if you mean 'promise' in the sense of 'guarantee,' I'm afraid it would be rather disingenuous of me to imply, er—"

"Look, Mr. Beeba," I interrupted, "just say yes, okay?"

He gave me a confused glance, then cleared his throat and spoke with a great show of confidence.

"Yes, of *course* I promise, Akiko. I promise, I *promise*."

"Thanks."

We stepped off the end of the bridge and into the blanket of snow covering the shore. There before us was the faint outline of a road stretching out over the hills.

The snow was thicker here by several inches, and it occurred to me that we might eventually have trouble following the trail. Not only that, but we had nowhere to spend the night! Surely we couldn't just sleep out in the open. But we couldn't keep walking all night, either. My head was starting to hurt and I began to really wish I were back at home in my bed, tucked under the covers, where I could just lean over, turn out the light, and—

GRRUMMMMMMMMMMMMMMMM!

Suddenly there was this horrible rumbling sound in the sky above us. At first I thought it was thunder, but then I realized that the noise was getting steadily louder and more mechanical sounding.

"I'd know that noise anywhere," Spuckler said. "It's a Gotgazzer!"

"A Gotgazzer!" Mr. Beeba repeated, searching the skies frantically.

"What's a Gotgazzer?" I asked.

"It's a kind of spaceship . . . ," Spuckler began.

Whatever he said after that was drowned out by the noise, which had now become so loud that Spuckler, Mr. Beeba, and I had to clamp our hands firmly over our ears. Gax was quivering, and Poog had floated down until he was nearly touching the ground.

A large black shape descended slowly from the sky in

front of us. Bolts of flame shot out beneath it, allowing the ship to settle gently onto the ground like an enormous dragonfly. The snow whirled madly in all directions, preventing me from getting a good view of the thing. Then the rumbling abruptly stopped, leaving a weird humming sound in my ears.

The clouds of snow gradually disappeared into the air, and I could see the spaceship clearly for the first time. It was about thirty feet wide and curved like a boomerang, with the steely gray surface of an armored submarine. There were several different kinds of guns mounted on the wings, and a big round window in front that looked like it could have been taken from one of those gigantic old warplanes you always see in the movies. The entire surface had a dull shimmer, as if it had been carefully polished for years and years.

Suddenly a horrifying thought dawned on me: Throck! This was Throck's spaceship, and he was coming out to confront us face to face.

My knees started shaking and the hairs on my neck stood up like the quills of a porcupine. My heart began to pound furiously, and I found myself breathing in

short, frightened gasps. I'd never been so scared in all my life.

"Come on, Throck," Spuckler whispered between clenched teeth. "Get out here and face us like a man."

Gax began to shudder uncontrollably, and Mr. Beeba inched his way behind me, poking his head out like a kid hiding behind a tree. Poog, however, rose high into the air and stayed right where he was, floating calmly and proudly as if he wasn't the least bit scared.

KA-CHAK!

There was a loud clicking sound as a door on top of the spaceship was unlatched.

FFSSSSSSSSSSSSSSSSSH!

It was that sound! The horrible sound of Throck's suit, pumping gas out into the air like an old steam engine.

Slowly, menacingly, Throck's head rose from the portal, his features lit from below with a greenish white light, allowing me to see his face clearly for the first time. His white hair stuck up from his head like the bristles of a scrub brush, cropped short on top, shaved to the scalp on the sides. His eyes were narrow and widely spaced, with tiny pale pupils, like the eyes of a snake. His cheeks were covered with tiny scars that looked like the stitching on a baseball. His nose and mouth were hidden by the same metallic cup we'd seen him wearing before. I guess he needed it to breathe, like a scuba diver on the depths of the ocean floor.

He continued climbing out of the ship until he was standing on one of the wings. Then he leaped off and landed on the ground with a muffled thump, momentarily losing his balance, then regaining it with a

strange, mechanical snapping motion. His arms and legs were a mass of tubes and canisters, his chest crisscrossed with dozens of creepy wires and pieces of armor. He stood there glaring at us for a minute or two, the hissing sound of his uniform piercing the air every few seconds.

"How many warnings will it take," his husky voice growled, "before you do as you are told?"

Chapter 25

Throck's cheeks rippled like the gills of a bloated fish as he waited for an answer.

"We don't need warnin's from the likes of *you*, pal," Spuckler said, stepping forward without hesitation. "We're on our way to Alia Rellapor's castle, and there ain't nothin' you can do t' stop us."

"My, my, little man," Throck said with a nasty chuckle, "you're a *brave* one, aren't you?" He leaned over to look Spuckler directly in the eyes. I felt a chill shoot straight down my spine.

"I usually find bravery a very admirable characteristic," Throck continued, his raspy voice just barely held above a whisper, "but your little show of bravado strikes me as rather sad. Have you any idea of the danger you're in?"

"Look, Throck—" Spuckler began.

"Well, well!" Throck interrupted, his eyes open wide in surprise. "How is it that you know my name? Not that it is of any *importance* to me . . ."

"We know *all* about you, Throck," Spuckler lied. "Now I suggest you step out of our way before I—"

"Before you *what?*" Throck interrupted again, this time barking the words like an angry dog. His face was now so close to Spuckler's that they were nearly touching.

Gax gave out a little

high-pitched whine, followed by a series of agitated clicks.

"Throck," Spuckler said in his most patient voice, "I'm gonna give you till the count of three to get outta here an' leave us alone."

There was nothing but silence.

"One . . ."

HISSSSSSSSSSSS!

A cloud of steam rose eerily from behind Throck's head.

"Two . . ."

"Time's up!" Throck growled, clamping his hands around Spuckler's waist. In one swift, graceful movement, he lifted Spuckler off the ground and threw him into the snow like a rag doll. Spuckler rolled when he hit the ground and scrambled to get back on his feet as quickly as he could.

Throck darted over to him with three quick strides of his enormous legs. Spuckler tried to throw a punch but ended up missing by a matter of inches. Throck snapped his hands around Spuckler's chest and tossed him at least twenty feet in the air. This time when Spuckler hit the ground he stayed right where he was, half buried in the snow.

I couldn't take it anymore. I ran over to where Spuckler lay and threw my arms around him. I pulled him up as best I could so that his head rested in my lap. Spuckler looked up at me for a moment, his eyes half open, half closed. He looked frighteningly weak.

"Leave him alone!" I shouted at Throck as loudly as I could. I felt a single hot tear run down my cheek. My face was burning up and my heart was pounding like crazy, but not so much out of fear, more just because I was so . . . I don't know, *awake*.

Throck stood where he was and scowled at me.

"You have no one to blame but yourselves,"

he sneered. "You saw the signs. You chose to ignore them."

Just then Poog began to float out toward me and Spuckler. He stayed with us for a moment, then turned and floated right up to Throck, finally coming to a stop about three feet in front of his face.

Poog was frowning. I'd never seen him look like that before. It was as if he were turning into an entirely different kind of Poog. He looked angry. *Really* angry.

It got very, very quiet. Even Throck's suit seemed to hiss less loudly.

The two of them stayed right where they were, Poog

staring at Throck, Throck staring at Poog. The tension between them was so strong you could almost *hear* it. And the weird thing was . . .

. . . *Throck* was the one who looked scared.

His eyes were open wide, his pale pupils quivering slightly. He seemed to require all his strength just to remain standing.

I'm not exactly sure, but I think I heard Throck *say* something to Poog. I don't know, it could have been just a cough, or the sound of his clearing his throat. But I think he *did* say something. If he did, then Poog simply chose to ignore him, because Poog stayed quiet the whole time, with a very cold, very *determined* look on his face. Nobody moved an inch.

Suddenly Throck turned away from Poog and walked back toward his ship. Mr. Beeba, who had watched the confrontation between Poog and Throck with ever-increasing interest, looked as if his jaw would hit the ground.

Throck climbed back up to the portal he'd come from just minutes before. He then turned to face us all one last time.

"Think long and hard about what you're getting yourselves into," he said slowly and clearly, as if he were trying to carve the words into our brains, "because once you've reached Alia Rellapor's castle . . ."

He paused for what seemed like a full minute.

". . . there will be no turning back."

Chapter 26

Throck's spaceship rocketed up into the night with a blinding flash of light. I've never been so happy to see someone go.

We all huddled around Spuckler, worried that he'd suffered some kind of deadly injury. Gax seemed especially concerned; he was making all sorts of rattling and beeping sounds, as if he was very, very nervous. Soon, though, Spuckler was sitting up and talking again, acting as if nothing had happened.

"I jus' got the wind knocked outta me, tha's all," he said, sounding slightly embarrassed about how quickly

Throck had defeated him. "Next time I'll give ol' Throck a taste of his own medicine!"

Mr. Beeba and I looked at each other and smiled.

When Spuckler had regained a bit of his energy, Mr. Beeba and I helped him to his feet. We walked him around in circles a couple of times, and before long he seemed to be back to normal.

Poog was off by himself, still staring into the sky where Throck's ship had disappeared. His face was tightened up into a look of great concentration, as if he was very deep in thought. I couldn't help wondering what he was thinking about, and I was dying to know what Throck had said to him. My mind was full of questions, but I decided to save them for later. We had other things to worry about.

The snow had started to let up a bit, but we were still stuck without a place to sleep. The sky was now pitch-black, and it looked as if we'd have no choice but to keep walking straight through the night. It was *not* a very pleasant idea.

"Wait a minute!" Mr. Beeba said, snapping his fingers. "The bridge!"

"What about it?" Spuckler asked.

"It'll be the perfect shelter," Mr. Beeba said, scampering back through the snow to where we had just come from.

"Come on, 'Kiko," Spuckler said, smiling. "I think I know what Beebs has in mind."

Spuckler, Gax, Poog, and I all followed Mr. Beeba down the snow-covered seashore alongside the bridge. A large section of beach was partially enclosed by some stone pillars that held up the bridge. Mr. Beeba led us underneath the bridge and into a little cavelike space that was almost completely cut off from the snow. It was still pretty cold, but at least we had some kind of roof over our heads. We all sat down and tried to get used to the idea of spending the night in such a dark, cold place.

"A li'l fire'll make this place a lot more homey," Spuckler said, pushing a button on Gax's body. Out came Gax's torch, with its bright, steady flame. Suddenly the frozen beach and the underside of the bridge were bathed in a warm yellow light. Spuckler was right. Just a simple thing like a bit of light made a pretty big difference.

That was just the beginning, though.

We all started gathering pieces of driftwood that had collected under the bridge. We put them all side by side and watched as Gax dried them with his torch. Some of them were pretty wet from all the ice and snow, and you could see steam rising into the air as Gax went to work on them. It took a while, but eventually Gax was able to make each piece of wood as dry as a bone.

Spuckler took the pieces of wood and carefully arranged them into a teepee shape. Then Gax stuck his

torch down at the bottom and set the whole thing aflame. Soon we were delighted to find ourselves huddled around a bright, crackling fire, warming our hands and feet and just generally making ourselves as comfortable as we could possibly be.

Then Spuckler pulled out the brown paper bag Yabby had given to us when we left his restaurant.

"Anyone hungry?" he asked.

Chapter 27

We stuffed ourselves with the sandwiches Yabby had packed for us. They were absolutely delicious, filled with all kinds of colorful vegetables and sweet slices of meat. There were also several purple pieces of fruit, and a whole bag full of Moolo Rings. We ate and ate and ate, devouring it all happily and *very* noisily.

After dinner we threw a few more pieces of wood on the fire so that Spuckler and Mr. Beeba could entertain us with hand shadows on the underside of the bridge. It was pretty amazing, all the different kinds of shapes they were able to make!

"Now, *this*, Akiko," Mr. Beeba explained, "is a frimbo

bird. I haven't *quite* got the wingspan right, but you get the general idea. . . ."

"And *this* is a flyin' saber-toothed mungasaurus," Spuckler growled, "comin' in to *eat* the frimbo bird!"

"Really, Spuckler!" Mr. Beeba chuckled. "Control yourself!"

They went on and on like that for more than half an hour. I even joined in here and there, making the shape of a dog's head and a couple of other tricks I learned from my uncle Koji back in Middleton.

After Spuckler and Mr. Beeba's little show was over, we all sat back and listened while Gax told a story about a giant spaceship he'd once been trapped on, and how he'd led a bunch of robots in a daring escape. He was really good at bringing the story to life, especially because he could make all sorts of cool sound effects as he went along. It was definitely the best robot story I'd ever heard. (Actually, it was the *only* robot story I'd ever heard, but you know what I mean.)

Finally Poog sang us a little song. It was a soothing, quiet song that seemed to wash over us like water, with beautiful airy sounds like flutes and strange, exotic harmonies that I could hear only if I tilted my head a certain way. Even with all the snow around, there was something very warm and almost tropical about the music.

Spuckler stoked the fire with plenty of wood so that it would keep us warm all night long. Gax said he'd add more wood later if the flames started to die down.

I suddenly found myself thinking about Throck, and the way Poog had stared at him, and the way he'd finally backed down and left us.

"Mr. Beeba," I whispered as I watched the firelight flicker on the underside of the bridge, "who do you think Throck *is*? Why is he trying to stop us from going to Alia Rellapor's castle?"

"Throck is as much of a mystery to me as he is to you, Akiko," said Mr. Beeba. "My guess is that he works for Alia Rellapor. He's probably been hired by her to prevent us from rescuing the Prince."

I sat and thought that one over for a minute. If this Throck guy was just an assistant, I wondered how scary *Alia* would turn out to be. Still, it was reassuring to know we had Poog around to protect us. It was almost like having a guardian angel at our side. If not for Poog, who *knows* what Throck might have done to us?

"You saw how Poog and Throck looked at each other, didn't you, Mr. Beeba?" I asked. "What do you think was going *on* there?"

"I'm not entirely sure, Akiko," he replied, "but I suspect that Poog and Throck have met before. Maybe once, maybe many times."

"Did you see the look on Throck's face?" I asked. "He looked really, really *scared*."

"He most certainly did," Mr. Beeba answered, "and I can't say I blame him. Poog has powers far beyond the likes of you and me. There's no telling what he's capable of doing in our defense."

I turned and looked at Poog. He was floating near the fire, and his eyes reflected the flames as clearly as pools of water. He was still humming to himself, and he wore an expression of deep, deep concentration. I wish I could have known what he was thinking, if only for a moment.

We all curled up in the warm sand near the edge of the fire and got ready to go to sleep. I found myself

looking back on everything we'd done in the past two days: our long walk through the grasslands, our perilous climb to the top of the Great Wall of Trudd, our delicious lunch at Yabby's restaurant . . . Some of it already felt as if it had happened a very long time ago.

"Sleep tight, everybody," Spuckler said as he folded his arms and rested his head on his chest. "Tomorrow we're goin' to Alia Rellapor's castle!"

What a thought to try to sleep on!

Our journey was nearly at an end. Would we really

make it to Alia's castle the next day? I wondered what the place would look like. I wondered what *Alia* would look like. And I wondered most of all if we'd really succeed in our mission to rescue Prince Froptoppit. I thought all the way back to when I had first come to the planet Smoo, and how King Froptoppit had put me in charge of rescuing his son. In my mind, I suddenly had a very clear image of the King with his lanky arms, oversized ears, and enormous white mustache.

"I need you to be in charge of this mission," he'd said to me that night. "And what's more, *you* need you to be in charge of this mission."

The fire crackled and popped, and I rolled over to warm the other side of my body. My head was filled with all kinds of questions. Normally I'd never have been able to fall asleep with so many things left to think about. But I was very tired, and my eyelids felt very, very heavy, and I knew that once I closed my eyes I'd be asleep in a matter of seconds. I took one last look at the firelight flickering across the beach as my eyelids slowly dropped over my eyes.

It was time to rest. We had a *very* big day ahead of us.

The adventure concludes in

in the Castle of Alia Rellapor

SEE WHERE IT ALL BEGAN:

Join Akiko and her crew on the Planet Smoo!

When fourth-grader Akiko comes home from school one day, she finds an envelope waiting for her. It has no stamp or return address and contains a *very* strange message. . . .

At first Akiko thinks the message is a joke, but before she knows it, she's heading a rescue mission to find the King of Smoo's kidnapped son, Prince Frop-toppit. Akiko, the head of a rescue mission? She's too afraid to be on the school's safety patrol!

Read the following excerpt from *Akiko on the Planet Smoo* and see how the adventure begins.

Chapter 1

My name is Akiko. This is the story of the adventure I had a few months ago when I went to the planet Smoo. I know it's kind of hard to believe, but it really did happen. I swear.

I'd better go back to the beginning: the day I got the letter.

It was a warm, sunny day. There were only about five weeks left before summer vacation, and kids at school were already itching to get out. Everybody was talking about how they'd be going to camp, or some really cool amusement park, or whatever. Me, I knew I'd be staying right here in Middleton all summer, which was just fine by me. My dad works at a company where they hardly ever get long vacations, so my mom and I have kind of gotten used to it.

Anyway, it was after school and my best friend, Melissa, and I had just walked home together as always. Most of the other kids get picked up by their parents or take the bus, but Melissa and I live close enough to walk to school every day. We both live just a few blocks away in this big apartment building that must have been built about a hundred years ago. Actually I think it used to be an office building or something, but then somebody cleaned it up and turned it into this fancy new apartment building. It's all red bricks and tall windows, with a big black fire escape in the back. My parents say they'd rather live somewhere out in the suburbs, but my dad has to be near his office downtown.

Melissa lives on the sixth floor but she usually comes up with me to the seventeenth floor after school. She's got three younger brothers and has to share her bedroom with one of them, so she doesn't get a whole lot of privacy. I'm an only child and I've got a pretty big bedroom all to myself, so that's where Melissa and I spend a lot of our time.

On that day we were in my room as usual, listening to the radio and trying our best to make some decent card houses. Melissa was telling me how cool it would be if I became the new captain of the fourth-grade safety patrol.

"Come on, Akiko, it'll be good for you," she said. "I practically promised Mrs. Miller that you'd do it."

"Melissa, why can't somebody *else* be in charge of the safety patrol?" I replied. "I'm no good at that kind of stuff. Remember what happened when Mrs. Antwerp gave me the lead role in the Christmas show?"

Melissa usually knows how to make me feel better about things, but even she had to admit last year's Christmas show was a big disaster.

"That was different, Akiko," she insisted. "Mrs. Antwerp had no idea you were going to get stage fright like that."

"It was worse than stage fright, Melissa," I said. "I can't believe I actually forgot the words to 'Jingle Bells.'"

"This isn't the Christmas show," she said. "You don't

It was all I could do to keep Melissa from snatching the letter from me once my mom was out of sight. She kept stretching out her hands all over the place like some kind of desperate basketball player, but I kept twisting away, holding the envelope against my chest with both my hands so she couldn't get at it.

"It's from a boy, isn't it? I knew it, I knew it!" she squealed, almost chasing me across the room.

"Melissa, this is *not* from a boy," I said, turning my back to get a closer look at the thing. My name was printed on the front in shiny black lettering, like it had been stamped there by a machine. The envelope was made out of a thick, glossy kind of paper I'd never seen before. There was no stamp and no return address. Whoever sent the thing must have just walked up and dropped it in our mailbox.

"Go on! Open it up!" Melissa exclaimed, losing patience.

I was just about to, when I noticed something printed on the back of the envelope:

TO BE READ BY AKIKO AND NO ONE ELSE

"Um, Melissa, I think this is kind of private," I said, bracing myself. I knew she wasn't going to take this very well.

"What?" She tried again to get the envelope out of my hands. "Akiko, I can't believe you. We're best friends!"

I thought it over for a second and realized that it wasn't worth the weeks of badgering I'd get if I didn't let her see the thing.

"All right, all right. But you have to promise not to tell anyone else. I could get in trouble for this."

I carefully tore the envelope open. Inside was a single sheet of paper with that same shiny black lettering:

DEAR AKIKO:
    WE ARE COMING
TO GET YOU. MEET US
OUTSIDE YOUR BEDROOM
WINDOW TONIGHT AT
8:00. DON'T FORGET
YOUR TOOTHBRUSH.

And that's all it said. It wasn't signed, and there was nothing else written on the other side.

"Outside my window? On the seventeenth floor?"

"It's got to be a joke." Melissa had taken the paper out of my hands and was inspecting it closely. "I think it *is* from someone at school. Probably Jimmy Hampton. His parents have a printing press in their basement or something."

"Why would he go to so much trouble to play a joke on me?" I said. "He doesn't even *know* me." I had this strange feeling in my stomach. I went over to the window and made sure it was locked.

"Boys are weird," Melissa replied calmly. "They do all kinds of things to get your attention."

Next, travel to the Sprubly Islands!

The mission to save Prince Froptoppit continues! Unfortunately, something happens to Akiko and her crew on the way to Alia Rellapor's castle. They get lost—hopelessly lost—in their flying boat somewhere over the Moonguzzit Sea. Their only chance is to find Queen Pwip of the Sprubly Islands, a clairvoyant who can point them in the right direction. As Akiko, Mr. Beeba, Spuckler, Gax, and Poog attempt to locate the queen, they must survive a skugbit storm, make their way out of the belly of a giant sea snake, and sail the seas to safety. But the Sprubly Islanders aren't at all like Akiko's friends and neighbors back on Earth. When Spuckler and Mr. Beeba disappear one night, Akiko is left to fend for herself in this strange and magical new world.

Read the following excerpt from *Akiko in the Sprubly Islands* and continue the adventure.

Chapter 1

I opened my eyes. I'd been sleeping so soundly that for the first few seconds I had no idea where I was. Then it slowly came back to me: I was on the planet Smoo with my new friends Spuckler Boach, Gax, Mr. Beeba, and Poog. We were floating peacefully above the clouds on our little flying boat, resting up before the next leg of our journey.

I was a little embarrassed to notice that everyone else was already awake. Mr. Beeba was steering the boat, Poog was floating quietly by himself just behind the mast, and Spuckler was giving Gax a little tune-up. (After all that poor robot had been through lately, I'm sure he needed it.)

"Hey there, Akiko," said Spuckler, smiling as always. "How ya doin'? Feels good to get a little shut-eye, don't it?"

"Yeah," I said, yawning and stretching my arms. "How long was I asleep?"

"Not *particularly* long," Mr. Beeba said, turning his head to join the conversation. "You've nothing to be ashamed of, dear girl. I would encourage you to get all the rest you can."

"Yeah, 'Kiko," Spuckler agreed. "'Cause there ain't nothin' *else* to do on this boat."

"You have *entirely* misconstrued the meaning of my statement, Spuckler," Mr. Beeba said wearily.

"I'm *right*, though," Spuckler insisted.

"You most certainly are *not*," Mr. Beeba answered. He was never one to pass by a good argument with Spuckler. And who was I to stop him? Watching the two of them go at it was as good as any television show. Poog was interested too, apparently. He floated over and gave himself a good view of the debate.

"I'm sure there are any *number* of interesting activities

2

for an intelligent child like Akiko to do on a boat such as this," Mr. Beeba continued.

"Name two," Spuckler grunted, tightening a bolt on Gax's underside.

"Well," Mr. Beeba began, "she could practice memorizing the names of all the books I've written—"

"That don't count," Spuckler interrupted. "You said *interesting*."

"She could follow *that* up," Mr. Beeba continued, ignoring Spuckler for the moment, "by memorizing passages from the books themselves."

"Well, that just proves my point," said Spuckler victoriously. "There ain't nothin' for 'Kiko to do on this boat but *sleep*." Gax clicked and whirred quietly as Spuckler tightened another bolt underneath his helmet.

"Hmpf!" Mr. Beeba snorted, apparently losing interest in the argument. There was a long pause, during which neither of them said anything. I found myself staring at the clouds and secretly agreeing with Spuckler.

After a long while I saw some orange-winged crea-tures flying overhead. They were the same creatures I'd seen way back when we'd just begun our journey.

"Hey, look, Mr. Beeba," I said, pointing up at them as they passed over us. "There's some more of those reptile-bird things you were telling me about before."

"Yumbas, Akiko. *Yumbas*," he replied, sounding slightly disappointed that I hadn't remembered the name. "An odd species, actually. All Yumbas fly in pre-cisely the same direction by instinct. Northeast, I believe. Or was it southwest? Well, in any case, it is said that the average Yumba literally circles the planet once every fourteen days."

"No kidding," I said, shielding my eyes from the sun as I watched the Yumbas fly off into the distance. "Where I come from, birds fly in pretty much any direction they want." I thought for a moment about my science teacher, Mrs. Jackson, back at Middleton Elementary. She had this big lesson plan one time about birds and how they fly south in the winter. She actually took us out into the school yard so that we could see real birds flying south. We didn't end up seeing anything, though, and all I remember is how cold it was and how I wanted to get back into the classroom as quickly as possible.

I leaned back on my elbows and looked up at the clouds again, wondering what direction the Yumbas were flying in. I wondered if they got tired of seeing the same scenery over and over again.

Then a really weird thing happened. A second flock of Yumbas passed overhead, and I thought for sure they were crossing over us in a slightly different direction. The time before, they had come from the left-hand side of the ship and had flown across to the right. This time it was just a little more from the front of the ship, heading toward the back. I sat there and waited to see if more Yumbas would pass overhead.

Sure enough, another group flew over us, and this time it was even more obvious that they were changing direction.

"Hey, Mr. Beeba," I said, "I think you might be wrong about those Yumbas."

"Me?" Mr. Beeba asked, as if I'd just proposed something altogether impossible. *Wrong?*

"It's nothing personal, Mr. Beeba," I explained cautiously. "I just think that maybe sometimes they fly in more than one direction."

"*Really*, Akiko," Mr. Beeba clucked disapprovingly. "It's one thing to postulate a theory contrary to my own, but quite another to do so without offering any proof whatsoever to back it up."

"Well, look up there and see what I'm talking about," I said, pointing at yet another group of Yumbas in the sky. Mr. Beeba coughed, cleared his throat, and watched as they passed over us, this time coming a little from the right and heading slightly to the left.

There was a long, awkward silence as Mr. Beeba followed the path of the Yumbas with his eyes.

"Inconceivable!" he said at last, scratching agitatedly at his head. "Yumbas *never* change direction."

"Now, wait a gol-darned second here," Spuckler said, jumping to his feet.

Mr. Beeba and I turned around to face him, a little surprised that he had any interest whatsoever in the conversation. Spuckler paced back and forth across the deck, looking up at the clouds and down at the Moonguzzit Sea beneath us, a very grim expression coming over his face. Gax watched him nervously, as if experience had taught him to be prepared for sudden drastic changes in Spuckler's mood.

"Those birds ain't changin' directions," he announced. "*We* are!"

"Us?" Mr. Beeba asked, his eyes widening. "You mean the *ship*? Don't be ridiculous!" There was a slightly uneasy sound in his voice, though, as if some terrible truth had just begun to dawn on him.

"We're goin' around in *circles* is what we're doin',"

Spuckler said, now starting to sound angry. "No *wonder* we been flyin' all this time and we still ain't past the Moonguzzit Sea!"

"F-flying in circles?" Mr. Beeba stuttered. "Nonsense! I've been steering this ship in an absolutely straight line!"

"You don't get it, do ya, Beebs?" Spuckler exclaimed, throwing his arms up in the air. "We are lost! *L-A-W-S-T*, lost!"

"We . . . ," Mr. Beeba began, trying rather desperately to defend himself, "we'd have *finished* this mission

by now if your Sky Pirate friends hadn't destroyed all my books!"

"Aw, you an' your stupid books!" Spuckler said. He was actually kind of shouting. "You ain't in your cozy little *library* anymore, Beebs. This is *reality* out here— take a good look!"

This argument seemed more serious than the little spats I'd seen so far, and I figured if I didn't interrupt they'd end up throwing punches or something. I cleared my throat and jumped in between the two of them.

"Look, we're never going to get anywhere if you two don't stop *arguing* all the time!"

Without even a pause, they stopped, turned, pointed at each other, and said (at exactly the same time), "*He* started it."

Honestly! You'd think they were first-graders or something.

"I don't care *who* started it," I said, putting on my best bossy voice and wagging a finger in front of both of them. "I'm in charge of this mission and I *order* you to stop fighting."

And it worked, too. They both got quiet and just

stared at the deck for a minute. A soft breeze blew over us and flapped through the sails as I allowed the silence to continue a little bit longer. The sun was getting lower in the sky, and we were all covered in a warm yellow glow.

"All right," I said finally. "We're going to sit right down here and have a little meeting."

"A meetin'?" Spuckler asked, with obvious disapproval.

"Yes. We're going to talk about how we got into this mess. Then we're going to find a way out of it." This was a little trick I'd learned from my history teacher, Mr. Moylan, back at Middleton Elementary. He said you always need to have a little meeting like this whenever you're in a tough situation and you can't figure out what to do next. Under the circumstances I think he'd have agreed this was a pretty good time to follow his advice.

ABOUT THE AUTHOR AND ILLUSTRATOR

Mark Crilley was raised in Detroit, where his parents sometimes wondered if he wasn't from another planet. After graduating from Kalamazoo College in 1988, he traveled to Taiwan and Japan, where he taught English to students of all ages for nearly five years. It was during his stay in Japan in 1992 that he created the story of Akiko and her journey to Smoo. First published as a comic book in 1995, the bimonthly Akiko series has since earned Crilley numerous award nominations, as well as a spot on *Entertainment Weekly*'s "It List" in 1998. *Akiko on the Planet Smoo*, Crilley's first work of fiction for young readers, was published by Delacorte Press.

Mark Crilley lives with his wife, Miki, and their son, Matthew, just a few miles from the streets where he was raised.